W9-AEC-651

DO OR DIE

Also by Grace F. Edwards

In the Shadow of the Peacock

If I Should Die

A Toast Before Dying

No Time to Die

DO OR DIE

A Mali Anderson Mystery

Grace F. Edwards

Doubleday
*New York London Toronto
Sydney Auckland*

PUBLISHED BY DOUBLEDAY
a division of
Random House, Inc.
1540 Broadway, New York, New York 10036

DOUBLEDAY and the portrayal of an anchor with a
dolphin are trademarks of Doubleday,
a division of
Random House, Inc.

This novel is a work of fiction. Names, characters,
places, and incidents either are the product of the
author's imagination or are used fictitiously. Any
resemblance to actual persons, living or dead, events,
or locales is entirely coincidental.

Book design by Dana Leigh Treglia

Edwards, Grace F (Grace Frederica)
Do or die: a Mali Anderson mystery/Grace F.
Edwards.—1st ed.

ISBN 0-385-49248-0

Printed in the United States of America

For my daughter

Perri and my

granddaughter Simone

Acknowledgments

My sincere thanks to my editor, Janet Hill, and Barbara Lowenstein, my agent, for having faith.

To the members of Harlem Writers Guild, especially William Banks, Sheila Doyle, Betty Ann Jackson, Alphonso Nicks, Diane Richards, and Sarah Elizabeth Wright, I owe you a lot. And to special HWG member Donis Ford; I thank you again for your long-distance friendship, insight, and expertise.

DO OR DIE

Dad could have taken the limo home as he sometimes does after a gig but since I was with him, he wanted to walk. And since he was so angry, he needed to talk.

The air at 4 A.M. held a close, almost sweet smell, not like the salty mist that had bathed us yesterday when we'd leaned over the port-side railing of the *QE2.* I usually noticed this sweet fragrance after a heavy downpour but it had not rained, at least not since we'd returned to New York.

Late yesterday afternoon we'd stepped from the gangway of a jazz cruise and Dad, after jamming on board and at the Newport Jazz Festival for the last seven days, had grabbed a few hours sleep, then showered, dressed, and left for his regular gig at the Club Harlem.

Music is my father's life but I don't want it to be the death of him. He's in his sixties and I see small nicks of fatigue cutting into the smoothness of his dark handsome face. Lines that weren't there yesterday seemed to have incubated overnight around the edge of his smile. I once suggested (and only once) that he try to slow down, and he huffed and puffed and nearly blew me through the wall.

"Slow down? Hell no. Lionel Hampton's old as water and still moving. Cecil Payne's still blowing baritone and Max Roach's still on the skins. Give me a break, Mali!"

Which I did. And said nothing when he left for the gig, but an hour later, I showed up at the club just to keep an eye on him. At the first hint of exhaustion, I had intended to drag him off stage, even if he killed me when we got home, but he and his guys sailed through both sets, smiled through the applause, and afterward moved easily through the crowd.

"Good show, Anderson," someone called. "You keepin' it real."

"Thanks, man."

"Glad you guys are back, Jeffrey. Now we can hear what jazz is all about."

Dad smiled at this, genuinely pleased. I followed in his wake as he pushed his bass toward the door. Outside the club, the lights lining the canopy dimmed and then went out, bathing the corner of Lenox Avenue and 133rd Street in a mottled gray.

The crowd, reluctant to give up the night, hung tight, looking for other places to greet the dawn. There was more handshaking. And some questions.

"Your man Hendrix was a no-show. So was his daughter. What's up with that? Too much *QE2*?"

"Tired, I guess," my father replied. "Ozzie went to cop some zee's and probably overslept. You know how that is."

His voice was steady but I watched the knot of annoyance taking shape in his lower jaw and I stepped up quickly.

"It was a great trip." I smiled. "Now Dad's gonna lay low for a few days."

"I hear what you sayin'. Gotta git your moves back. Check you on the weekend and hopefully your piano man, too."

Dad smiled wider, a genial, professional, crowd-pleasing beam, but inside, I knew he was steaming.

Ozzie Hendrix, whom Dad had known for nearly forty years, through the blues, bop, and jazz scenes, was the pianist. He and Dad had crisscrossed at cabarets in the Village, studio sessions, Fifty-second Street clubs, one-night stands, and every after-hours joint that had room for a combo. A few years ago, they hooked up seriously when Dad put the ensemble together for the club. Ozzie had amazing technical skill and his fingers on the keys transported a listener to the very soul and center of his music. Dad with his bass set the rhythm and kept the pace, but it was Ozzie with his artistry, his virtuoso technique, who usually brought the crowd to its feet.

We turned off Malcolm X Boulevard and into the quiet of 133rd Street, heading toward Powell Boulevard. We walked slow. Dad talked fast. I tried not to interrupt, preferring to concentrate instead on the delicate 4 A.M. stillness and the wheel of his bass as it rolled over the sidewalk's pebbly surface. At the corner, the silence was fractured by a riff leaping from a passing car radio, muted somewhat because the driver had no one to impress. A transient interruption that instantly faded. Then from behind a fence somewhere came the long, low howl of a dog.

"... *When puppy cry, somebody die,*" Mom used to say, falling into the Charleston-Bajan cadence of *her* grandmother. My mom died years ago and so had my sister, Benin. After the initial shock and loneliness of losing someone you really love, you learn to listen in the silence and somehow they come back. They come back. Right now I missed Mom more than ever. She could've calmed Dad with a smile.

When I tuned in again, his anger had risen above everything.

"Never again, dammit! That's the last time I do anybody a favor. Don't care how tight we are. Give 'em a break and get screwed every damn time. And his daughter was supposed to be there tonight. The featured singer. Damn picture plastered on every poster in every store window in Harlem. And not only didn't she show but neither did he. And not a word. Least they coulda done was get on the drum. This way, the rest of us woulda known what we had to do!"

I breathed deeply and offered no comment as we turned into 139th Street, between Adam Clayton Powell Boulevard and Frederick Douglass Boulevard. Strivers Row, as folks called it. A block of three- and four-story neo-Italianate and Colonial revival rowhouses adorned with wrought-iron balconies and French windows that were now closed against the humid night air and, hopefully, the sound of Dad's anger.

We walked past 221, home of Vertner Tandy, the African-American architect who designed St. Phillips Episcopal Church and Madame C. J. Walker's mansion in Irvington-On-Hudson. I counted the doors until we passed number 228, where Fletcher

Henderson, the bandleader, once lived. While living here he was able to walk to his gigs at the jazz clubs just as Dad does now when he doesn't feel like calling for the limo.

Exhaustion hit me like a brick. Suddenly, seven days of tapping my foot to the beat of Aretha, Lou Rawls, Branford Marsalis, and Ruth Brown, and lounging in deck chairs until my skin was fried two shades past midnight, and each night wrapped in Tad's arms and rolling to his private and indescribable rhythm, and then rising to jog around the deck with him in a 5 A.M. fog, all had finally caught up with me. My eyelids felt like a sandpit. I was ready to tell Dad but he was still swimming in a current of anger.

"The last thing Ozzie said when we left the ship was 'See you tonight. Starr'll be there. I really appreciate what you doin' for her.' And neither one of 'em bothered to show. What the hell is that about? At this stage of the game, I damn sure don't need no half-steppers!"

I knew how Dad felt. If he was able to drag himself out of the house, then everyone else should've done it also. Or at least call. Luckily, a jazz pianist from Brooklyn was in the audience and was more than happy to sit in. And he was damn good. I listened and wondered how a musician—who had never played or practiced with a particular group—could simply walk on, take a seat, and blend so seamlessly with the rhythm, strike the notes as cleanly as if he'd gigged with the band for years.

I heard the ringing above Ruffin's bark as I put the key in the door.

"Maybe it's Alvin," I said. "You know we promised to call as soon as we got back."

"Or could be Ozzie," Dad said as he propped his bass against the sofa and rushed to the phone before the machine kicked in. "If it is, he better have a damn good—"

A second later, I watched the annoyance drain away and his

face change to blank surprise. His hand shook violently and he tried twice before finally hitting the speakerphone button.

Ozzie's voice cracked through the silence like an electric charge. "Bad news, man. Bad, bad. Starr's dead. My baby's been murdered."

2

It didn't take long to get over to Starr's place, a four-story apartment building on 122nd Street overlooking the grassy knoll of Marcus Garvey Park. Her apartment was on the second floor and at first, we were not allowed in the building.

The area had been secured and homicide detectives, crime scene technicians, and a photographer were present, as well as several uniforms trying to control the crowd milling around and adding to the confusion.

One homicide detective with the improbable name of Holmes moved through the lobby toward the door and recognized me from my time on the force. My tenure had been brief but memorable, like one of those meteors that appear out of nowhere, cause tremendous upheaval, and then exit into another orbit. Except that I hadn't exited altogether, as the mayor, the commissioner, and the precinct's captain had wished. I was still here, alive and well and still mad as hell.

"Your boy's upstairs," Holmes whispered, nodding his head toward the steps. He saw my hard stare and quickly understood that I was not acquainted with any forty-two-year-old "boys."

He also knew my history; knew I'd gotten fired for punching out a racist cop and that I'd sued the NYPD for wrongful dismissal. In the process, some rocks had been overturned at the precinct and more than one secret had been exposed to the light of day. Drug dealing, murder, and bribery headed the list. I had blown a hole in the setup and nearly brought down the entire precinct. When the smoke cleared, the cop I had punched was dead but my lawsuit continued. Now, to prevent me from testifying and bringing up all that unpleasant stuff, I was being offered an out-of-court settlement. Reinstatement at the rank of detective sergeant and immediate retirement on ninety percent disability. How could I refuse?

I was in the final stage of negotiations and I assumed Holmes did not want me running back to my attorney for a bonus. I stared at him and he promptly corrected himself. "I mean your . . . your guy, your friend is upstairs."

I did not reply and so to make further amends, he cupped his hand to his mouth, leaned on the banister and called, "Yo, Honeywell! Got a minute? Somebody's down here!" Then he clamped his jaw as if he were nursing a toothache and strode out toward the crime scene van.

Dad and I exchanged a look. Tad Honeywell. Tad was here. I couldn't believe it. We had been exhausted when we left the ship and he was going home to crawl under the covers. Then again, that's also what I'd planned to do, but Dad's gig had somehow gotten in the way.

I heard Tad's voice at the top of the stairs but on the way down, the medical examiner intercepted him and he turned and retraced his steps.

Up on the landing, a neighbor's door eased open and Ozzie, moving like a shadow, walked downstairs toward us. He and Dad were about the same age but whereas Dad was tall and thin, Ozzie had the hard, ageless physique of George Foreman. His sharp features now seemed melted in grief and his clean-shaven head glistened with sweat under the fluorescent hall light. He moved slowly, measuring each step like a man newly blind, fearful of stumbling into something unknown.

"I don't want to go too far," he whispered as Dad took his arm and we walked outside. Up close, I saw that his skin had lost the sun-deck, cruise-bronzed coloring and an ashen tinge had broken through.

"I don't want to go too far," he whispered again. "Don't want to leave her like that. She . . ."

We guided him across the street to a bench near the park. He held his head and we listened to his halting breath in the silence. Finally, he looked up and stared across the street. He gazed at the small crowd, the crime scene van, and the squad cars with their rotating lights disturbing the gray morning.

"You know, Jeffrey, I shoulda brought her on the trip. Just had her pack a bag and come on with us. This woulda never happened if she hadda been with me . . ."

"How did it happen?" I whispered. "Was it a break-in? Was she robbed?"

He hunched his shoulder and shook his head at an angle, as if a weight held it to one side. "Can't tell if anything's missing.

Didn't have time to look. I went to use the key she gave me, but the door was unlocked, closed but unlocked. Something was behind the door when I pushed. It was her, laid out, throat cut ear to ear."

He drew a deep breath and seemed to stop breathing for a second before he continued.

"She shoulda came with me. But no. Said she had to be here. Had some business she had to take care of. And look what happened. Look at what happened."

Look at what happened... He closed his eyes and repeated this slowly, as if in the repetition he might uncover some mistake, some error of the eye that would self-correct—she'd only been sleeping after all and eventually would awaken and make things whole again.

"I called her, soon as we cleared the deck," he continued. "No answer. Machine didn't kick in and I thought she mighta been in the shower or something. So I came straight here. Knew we didn't have much time and I wanted her to be ready for this gig. Especially for this gig. And I found her layin' there. Don't know how long she been dead. God, if I'd only been here. If I'd only . . ."

I glanced over his shoulder and caught my father's eye. His expression seemed to say, "Don't ask any more questions. Not now. He's not up to it."

I nodded and pointed toward the building, then left them and walked across the street. I eased around the crowd again, smaller now that most of the onlookers, disappointed that the body was not forthcoming, had wandered back to the double- and triple-locked security of their own homes. Some of the cruisers had also dispersed, leaving two cars to flash on the remaining spectators clustered in tight whispering knots.

Tad stood in the doorway of the building, talking in a low voice to one of the identifying technicians. I waited until the tech disappeared inside again before I signaled. Tad's face, when he approached, was like stone. His mouth was a fine, thin line and his eyes, usually pools so calm and deep I wanted to dive into them, were now narrowed and focused like a laser on this latest circumstance.

"How's Ozzie doing?" he asked.

"Not too well. Probably still in shock," I whispered, following his gaze across the street to the bench. Ozzie sat with his head resting against the iron railing and Dad sat next to him, whispering in a voice too low to carry on the humid air.

Spears of pale pink light were pushing through the gray and Ozzie appeared to be sleeping but I knew he wasn't. He nodded every now and then as Dad continued to speak. I'd find out later what he'd said. Right now, Tad was guiding me away from the nearby knot of onlookers.

We settled in the front seat of his favorite unmarked car, a battered Olds with molting paint and a loose spring in the front seat that let the passenger know that even the shortest ride was not meant to be a joy but one of serious butt-kicking official business.

He folded an old thick copy of the Sunday *Times* over the spring and I was able to slide in without too much damage to my hips.

"Any ideas?" I asked. My voice was soft in the closed space and he looked at me. I saw fatigue shade his eyes and he glanced through the window.

"Whoever did her in must've really had it in for her. The cut's so deep, it severed her windpipe and carotid artery and more than likely she bled to death in a matter of minutes."

I waited, wondering if he was going to tell me the rest. Things that I and some folks already knew.

"There're old track marks on her arms and the insides of her ankles."

"But she wasn't into that anymore," I said. "In fact, she'd turned her life completely around, had gotten herself together and was ready to sing at—"

"I know. There's a blowup of the poster in her living room. With an X slashed across it top to bottom."

"Damn. Somebody *was* mad."

He closed his eyes and shook his head and now with the smile gone I saw weariness catching up with him also.

"She may've started a new life, Mali, but sometimes it pays to settle some outstanding debts before closing the book."

I did not answer but wondered if that's what Ozzie meant.

She had some business, something she had to take care of...

Through the window, I watched the medical examiner step from the house and walk the few feet to his car. Then two other men—morgue attendants with latex-gloved hands ghost white against their dark work clothes—emerged carrying a canvas bag shaped like a small rolled carpet. Starr had been only five feet tall and inside the bag could have been the body of a child. The onlookers stirred and a young woman in the crowd started to cry. Then someone else, someone who'd probably known Starr or had heard her practicing—started to sing in a voice that was very old, then gave way to a hollow call. When the others joined in, the hollow echo filled out, thickened with grief.

I had one foot out of the car when I heard Ozzie cry out as if he were locked in a stranglehold. Then he sprang up from the bench, his eyes wide as if searching out the voice. And before Dad could catch him, he collapsed to the ground.

He had managed to sit up just as Tad and I reached him. Dad knelt down, steadying him.

"We're taking you to the hospital, Ozzie. You've had a terrible shock. You—"

"No. No, man. I'm . . . I'm all right. Just get me home. Just take me home."

We piled into Tad's car and drove west on 125th Street. At this hour, traffic was slow but smooth. I gazed out the window at the landscape of steel-shuttered stores and deserted sidewalks, streets that in a few hours would be dense with people. But even in the density, in the flow and rush of pedestrians, I knew there was an absence, a large hole lying like a presence just beneath the high-noon hustle. An absence so palpable it had become a presence to me.

I closed my eyes and listened to Ozzie's labored breathing above the whir of the tires. Part of me flitted away from him, back to the street, the crossroads of black America where, despite the feel-good political hoopla, those streets were not open to certain traffic. I gazed at the Apollo Theatre where Inner City Broadcasting was under seige by the politicians. Across from the theatre, Mart 125 was still battling to control their enterprise. The African street vendors had been swept away by the "Downtown Clown" in City Hall to parts unknown. Black America's crossroads with someone else directing the traffic. I felt the large hole growing larger.

I opened my eyes and gazed straight ahead. This was a hell of a time for political musing, but I suppose I did it to avoid the reality of Ozzie's nightmare. Two years ago, his wife had lost her battle with cancer. He had pulled his only child from a swamp of drugs only to lose her also. This time to murder. How could this have happened?

Ozzie was probably thinking the same thing as we pulled up in front of his house, a large brownstone situated between Manhattan and Morningside avenues two blocks from the old Sydenham Hospital. He occupied the parlor floor and garden level and had left the upper floor vacant, ready for Starr in case she ever needed to return.

His wife and daughter were gone. No one was coming back. Now he would be competely alone in this house.

Ozzie stood at the curb staring vacantly past the iron gate. His gaze traveled up to the top floor with its curtained windows and shades half drawn. "Well, I guess . . . I guess this is it. I suppose . . ."

Dad took his arm and led him through the gate and up the stairs.

"You two head on home," he said. "I'm gonna stay with him awhile. I'll see you later."

Tad nodded. Any further questions at this point would have been fruitless.

"Dad, call me if you need anything."

I kissed him and hugged Ozzie and returned to sit in the car. Daylight flooded everything now. Trees, shrubs, and planters, clipped and cultivated, bloomed behind high wrought-iron railings. Folks were opening doors, stepping out to a new August day, and moving in a steady stream toward the subway. The block was small and lovely and held a closed feeling of privacy, of tranquility. I listened to the birds chatter and wondered how a dream could have disintegrated so quickly and plunged us all into a nightmare.

A week earlier, we had been aboard ship and I was lounging in a deck chair scanning the flat Atlantic horizon. Calm sea. Bright sun breaking through scudding pink-tinted clouds. Tad was massaging a lavender-scented oil on my legs and concentrating so hard, I couldn't keep the smile from my face.

He had surprised me when he booked the jazz cruise, not only because Dad's group was scheduled to perform on board but also as a kind of therapy for me. He felt that I needed to get away, to try to forget the nightmare I'd just gone through with that serial killer who had terrified most of Harlem. The scars on my legs from the episode were still visible and Tad was determined to slowly smooth them away.

He looked up from his labors and whispered, "How we doin', baby? Need more lotion or more motion?"

I leaned over and tilted his visor so I could look into his sun-flecked eyes. Sometimes, he asked the damnedest questions. Most of the time he already had the answer. My fingers traced the edge of silver at his temples, then I kissed him quickly, without a word, and we left the deck, heading for the cabin, intending to explore this motion thing in more detail. He slipped the key in the door when someone called, "Going in so soon?"

I heard Tad murmur, "Oh, shit," as Chrissie Morgan strolled toward us clad in a see-through, knotted midriff blouse and a pair of pressure-resistant Daisy Dukes and not a varicose vein in sight on her fifty-year-old legs. The rest of her wasn't too bad either, what with her short-cut hair streaked gold to cover the gray and her green contacts glimmering in her cruise-tanned face.

Her stomach was flat as a board and she raised her hands casually to emphasize her ample hips. "You two aren't going to nap, are you? It's barely past noon."

"Ah, yes, Christine." Tad smiled. "Sun kinda got to us so we're gonna—"

"How about a round of poker. I could use a partner." Her voice was so low, I wondered if that tight bra had cut off her oxygen.

"We're rather tired," I interjected, dispensing with decorum. "Perhaps another time."

"Yes, perhaps." She looked at Tad and parted her mouth. The smile was large and off-center, like those of the portraits on the new money. Then she waved her hand and continued down the corridor.

Inside the cabin, I sprawled across the bed watching Tad mix two Bellinis.

"What's with that woman?" he said, handing me a tall frosted glass. "Just because we're all seated at the same dining table doesn't mean we're joined at the hip for the entire trip."

I sipped the peach-flavored champagne, offering no comment. I knew what her problem was. She hadn't been able to keep her eyes off Tad the minute he'd walked up the gangway. And at dinner the first night out, it had taken less than a minute for me to decide I couldn't stand her. An opinion confirmed when she had smiled at me and said, "What lovely eyes, but gray? A bit startling for your . . . uhm . . . for you."

I had felt the steady pressure of Tad's hand on my knee under the table, signaling me to ignore her. Hell no. Here she was, sporting contacts so filmy they looked like cataracts. Girl had more nerve than a bad tooth and I intended to fix her, tooth and all, in the first round.

"Some folks," I said slowly, "have had a problem with my gray eyes and dark complexion ever since I was born. I can't tell you what a joy it is to advise such stupid people to look the other way if they're so disturbed."

We had been seated at a table for eight and a discreet silence descended, broken only by the soft clink of soup spoons quietly dipping into bowls of consommé.

When it was safe for conversation to resume, she casually announced among other things that she was cruising as a single. "My girlfriend couldn't make it," she had murmured, "so I have the stateroom all to myself." Her eyes had flitted around the table, lighting on each man before settling like a moth on Tad.

Lying across the bed now, I wondered about her husband. Travis Morgan was well known in Harlem, a nice guy with a growing business selling and repairing computers. He was in his early forties, not bad-looking, a jazz lover who frequently dropped by the club. Why wasn't he with her on this trip?

The ship was due to dock in Bar Harbor the next day and I was looking forward to a shore dinner of Maine lobster—the real thing—with cole slaw and french fries and a king-sized napkin tucked under my chin to catch the drippings. I looked forward to drawn butter to dip the claws in. Even though the main meat was in the tail, I preferred the claws. Tad mixed another round of Bellinis and refilled my glass. Then he drew the curtains over the porthole and the cabin was suffused in a soft half-light. I felt the slow, undulating rhythm of the ship and watched as Tad moved toward me. For a brief second, I thought of Chrissie and hoped that before the cruise ended, I wouldn't have to dip my claws in her hide.

That was several days ago. Now I stood outside Ozzie's place and watched Dad lead him up the steps. The door closed behind them, shutting the world off from the grief I knew was coming. With no other relatives, it would probably fall to Dad to make the necessary arrangements: contact the undertaker, get the body released from the morgue, get in touch with friends and all the musicians Ozzie had played with.

On the way home, Tad detoured to Pan Pan's restaurant on 135th Street for breakfast. We ate silently, too tired to lift anything heavier than the waffles, bacon, sausage, and eggs. Talk was limited to "pass the biscuits, pass the butter, pass the check."

He dropped me off and I let myself into the house. Ruffin, our Great Dane, rose from his favorite spot near the fireplace, stretched, and approached with an accusatory look—reminding me that we had left him in our neighbor's care, retrieved him yesterday, only to desert him again for several hours when Ozzie called.

Even Alvin, my nephew, was away. He had chosen to spend the time on our friend Captain Bo's schooner in St. Croix rather than cruise on the *QE2.*

"Can I dive from the deck? Can I throw a line from the side? Can I hoist a sail?" he had asked, knowing very well that he could not.

When Dad had nodded, Alvin said, "Then I'd rather hang out with Captain Bo. Besides, if the *QE* ain't into hip-hop, I'm not interested."

"Isn't. *Isn't* into hip-hop," Dad had corrected. He had rolled his eyes toward the ceiling and was still rolling them when we'd waved Alvin off at Kennedy to spend the time with the Captain, Tad's friend who owned a ninety-foot, four-masted sailboat in St. Croix. Dad had fumed as we drove back from the airport. "Hip-hop! After all I've taught that boy about jazz . . ."

"Alvin's still a kid," Tad had said as he maneuvered through stop-and-slow traffic on the Grand Central Parkway. "He'll get through this stage and eventually come to appreciate what you're teaching him: that jazz is our religion, our heritage, our way of expressing who we are. He'll come to understand that."

I said nothing, but privately nursed a quiet disappointment. This was the vacation of a lifetime, with performers who might not even be around when Alvin got through his stage, whatever it was.

The cruise was over but Alvin was still away and the house seemed large in its emptiness. I picked up the phone and seconds later his voice came scratchily through a bad connection.

"Hey, Mali? What's goin' on?"

"Everything and nothing," I replied. "Just called because I miss you and wanted to hear your voice."

"How was the cruise? I know Grandpa was hangin' with the heavies. He make it through all right?"

"Of course he did. He's a pro himself," I said. "He was great."

"I knew it. I knew he'd do it." His voice faded into static again and I caught a fragment.

". . . home in two weeks, okay?"

"Two weeks? You'll be home?"

"Yeah. Fishin's great. Swimmin's great. Weather's fine. This is the bomb, man. I mean the bomb . . ."

More static and I caught something pertaining to hang time and had a vision of him swinging from the yardarm, so I said, "How's the captain?"

"Bo said hello. Wants to know when you guys are comin' down. I told him that after bein' on the *Queen*, this'll seem like small change."

"Oh, Alvin, you didn't." I had a vision of Bo canceling future invites. "Tell him we'd love to come, perhaps next summer, okay?"

"No problem. Gotta go. Tell Morris and Clarence hello if you run into 'em. Tell Grandpa I love him."

More static and he clicked off, leaving me alone again, conscious of the quiet that seemed to close in.

I wandered upstairs and lay across the bed, too tired to undress. Maybe I had gone beyond ordinary fatigue because for a time I seemed to float in a bodiless state somewhere between sleep and wakefulness, listening to a voice inside my head that would not turn off.

"Starlight, star bright, first star I see tonight..."

Ozzie had named his daughter Starr because, he said, she was destined to be one. She was three years younger than me but had always acted at least three years older. We hadn't been particularly close, so she had grown in my imagination through Dad's friendship with her father.

As a child, she had come to the house with Ozzie from time to time and instead of hanging with me, she had preferred to sit in on rehearsals. There, she learned to handle a mike probably before she learned to properly handle a fork. While other girls I knew were sewing doll clothes, Starr was making stage costumes for herself.

When she was eleven, she sang at the Apollo and even though she didn't win, she didn't exactly lose either. Dad said anyone who made it through without getting the hook from the Sandman should consider herself a winner. Ozzie had bought tickets for us all and had later taken us to Snookies Sugar Bowl, where we forgot about the Apollo the minute those double dark chocolate ice cream sundaes had been placed before us.

I remembered how she had been blessed with a childlike beauty: a small frame, a round dark brown face with doll-like features that folks said would remain the same no matter how old she'd get. But she didn't live long enough to prove it one way or the other. She'd had business to take care of, Ozzie said. And someone instead had managed to take care of her. She didn't live to see her twenty-eighth birthday.

Hours later, I rolled over and stared at the clock on the night table: 5 P.M. I had been more tired than I thought. A cool shower and two cups of coffee revived me enough to collar Ruffin and walk to Frederick Douglass Boulevard. I needed to see my beautician—not to have my two-inch Afro tended, but to find out if she'd heard anything about Starr.

Bertha, my twenty-year friend, owns Bertha's Beauty Salon and is a reliable source of street news, gossip, and any scandal worth repeating. She has been at the same location on Eighth Avenue years before it was renamed for Frederick Douglass and she doesn't have to poke her head out the door to catch a whisper. It flows in automatically as early as 7 A.M., when the regulars from Miss Laura's luncheonette arrive with breakfast and news hotter than the grits. This is the early edition, followed by periodic updates. Then the after work crowd wraps it up in the evening.

Bulletins, like who caught a digit, who got busted with someone else's spouse, or who didn't survive a shootout, come in immediately. For bulletins, Bert sacrifices the soaps and turns the TV not down, but off completely.

On Saturdays, she supplements the hot oil treatments and deep conditioners with "The Week in Review Special."

I had been away seven days, So I was in desperate need of the Review.

When I walked in, she was twisting the last row of Senegalese braids on her customer's head, shaping the hair like a finely sculpted tiara. I had tied Ruffin to the parking meter and took a seat near the window in order to keep an eye on him.

"Girl, look at you!" Bertha said. "First time I ever seen a dark person get a tan. Your eyes look like traffic lights."

The woman in the chair peered in my face, blinked, and glanced away. I half expected her to make the sign of the cross to ward off the evil that was sure to come her way, but I said hello and she managed a weak smile.

Before I could get comfortable in the chair, Bert said, "I know you got a lot to tell, so start at the beginnin' and don't leave a comma out."

Her fingers flew along the deep furrows of the woman's hair, applying a light patina of shea oil to the scalp. Then she added three cowrie shells at the base of the tiara and removed the plastic capelet from the women's shoulders.

The woman studied herself in the wide mirror, paid generously for the transformation, and left smiling. She even waved good-bye in my direction.

"You had dinner yet?" Bert asked as she counted the dollars.

"I'm not hungry," I said, remembering the shipboard menus and the flourish with which the waiters presented them at the table. Diners were addressed as sir or madame with the accent on "dam'." The petite packets of Philadelphia Lite cream cheese were manufactured in Germany, and the sommelier wore a medallion heavy enough to anchor the ship in a hurricane.

I sighed myself back to reality, knowing that in a day or two the candlelit ambiance and the taste of filet mignon and escargot would be a dim memory, and fried chicken, collard greens, and red rice would once more loom large on the palate. Especially the collard greens.

"Then again," I said, "maybe I *am* a little hungry. What do you have in mind?"

"What else but Charleston's barbecued ribs and chicken with candied yams, red rice, and greens. He got delivery service now. Nuthin' fancy. Just some young brother hangs outside who Charleston got a bike for and put 'im to work. Just hiccup and I'm on the horn."

A half hour later, I bit into a crisp chicken leg and the tangy barbecue sauce obliterated everything related to cruise cuisine. Between bites, I described the jazz lineup: Lou Rawls's throaty voice floating over the crowd in the ship's two-tiered grand salon; the Milt Jackson Quartet, Slide Hampton's trombone, and Christian McBride's Quartet at the after-midnight jam session. James Moody, and of course, my dad's group, which played side by side with some of jazz's best innovators.

Bert listened, openmouthed, when I described how the audience rose to its feet when Ruth Brown strutted the stage in her sequined gowns and high heels and dished her down-home humor.

"She sing about her old antique chair?"

"You know she did. And she's still sitting on it. Said if she can't sell it, she ain't gonna give it away."

"Damn, the girl's all right. Sorry I missed that trip."

"And," I said, working my way through the red rice, "you should've heard Aretha riff with one of the Temptations at Newport."

"That's it! Next year, I'm goin' even if I have to close shop for two weeks. I'm missin' all this good stuff. Life's too short. Me and my honey is gonna be there."

Her face lit with anticipation and I smiled at this, at her sudden, surprising, and perfect happiness. One day last month, Bert had worked on Mrs. Gibson, an elderly woman from uptown, and had gotten her to smile in satisfaction when she had finished styling her hair. The woman's son came to pick her up and Mrs. Gibson, as plainspoken as Bertha, pointed to him as he walked in.

"This is Franklin, my son. Forty years old. Only thing wrong is a touch of diabetes. Otherwise he's perfect. Good eyesight, good upbringing, and good jay-oh-bee. Windower two years. Take my word for it 'cause I don't lie for nobody. Take his phone number too."

And Franklin, accustomed to his mother, had simply smiled, reached out, and shaken Bertha's hand. Bertha, for once in her life, had been too astounded to open her mouth.

Franklin was a shade under six feet, slim and brown, and had a smile, Bert saw, that was bright enough to chase blues a woman didn't even know she had.

The next day, he'd sent a dozen yellow roses with a card thanking her for the way she'd styled his mother's hair.

"You see that." Bert had smiled. "Any man who looks out for his mama will look out for you."

When he called for a date, Bert didn't have to think too hard or too long.

"How's Franklin?" I said, watching her smile widen.

"Doin' fine," she murmured. "Matter of fact, he just left here."

I nodded, watching her, and unable to believe that her voice actually dropped an octave when she mentioned his name.

"So what else happened?" she asked, changing the subject back to the cruise. "How'd your dad like it? Who else was aboard? Anybody from the neighborhood?"

"The trip would've been perfect," I said, "but I had the bad luck to be seated at the same table as Christine Morgan. Girl couldn't keep her eyes off Tad."

Bert looked up from her dinner plate, her mouth rounding to form a small *O*. "You kiddin'? Damn. That *is* bad! Wait a minute. I seen her hubbie last week. Drivin' by in that shiny Mercedes. You mean he didn't go with her?"

"No. And first night out, she announced in no uncertain terms, to every man at the table, that she was traveling solo. It was practically an invitation to her open house."

"Well, I can understand that. Me and Franklin was at the club, probably a few nights before you sailed. Travis was there, and Christine come huffin' in. Got all in his grille, accusin' him of steppin' with his 'other bitch,' as she put it."

"What?"

"Yep. Even though he was solo, the mama staged some drama. Before the waiters could rush her, she stormed the ladies' room, hopin' to jam the woman in there. Thank God it was empty but she musta scanned each booth like an inspector from the health department 'cause by the time she came out, Travis had paid his check and faded.

"Your pop upped the tempo 'til the tourists got tired of stretchin' their necks. You shoulda seen those cameras break out. Ready to snap a real Harlem happening. Something to take home to the folks. But she left after a while, probably tryin' to catch up with poor Travis some place else."

I frowned. "Maybe that's why she was alone on the cruise. That last-minute fight probably soured him and he canceled."

And, I thought, that's why she had strolled the deck in those outrageous outfits, ready to hit on any man whose shadow fell across her path.

Dad hadn't mentioned the scene at the club. And he certainly hadn't seemed uncomfortable when he found she had been assigned to our table. But then, a musician's life is not quiet. He's probably seen so much stuff that some things weren't worth mentioning. For a second, I felt a pocket of sympathy open within me. But it was a small pocket, not quite deep enough to make me forget her remark about my eyes. Then I remembered how she had eagle-eyed Tad and I concluded that she was still a bitch and the pocket zipped closed.

Bert dipped her last spare rib into the sauce and raised it to her mouth. "Miss Chrissie's uptight 'cause you know she's a bit older than Travis. But girlfriend also oughta know by now that age ain't nuthin' but a number."

"One would think so," I said. "What else did I miss?"

"Well, I know you know about Starr 'cause her daddy in your daddy's band. And it was all on the vine this morning."

"I know. We were at her place around four this morning. Whoever did it must have really had it in for her."

Bert shook her head. "You know, the good die young. That girl had a special voice. Coulda been the next Sarah Vaughn or somethin'. Talk has it that her throat was open ear to ear. If you ask me, I think somebody was jealous, didn't want her gittin' ahead. Or maybe it was Short Change. You know how low down he could get."

Short Change, I knew, was a pimp who'd once tried to recruit Starr and in the process had introduced her to a heroin habit that had dragged her through hell and back. Last summer, Ozzie had tracked Short Change and played taps on his skull with a metal pipe, played so hard no one expected him to recover, but somehow he did. Now Ozzie would probably be looking for him again.

"Well," Bert said as she folded her empty carton into a plastic garbage bag, "if I was Short Change, I'd be pullin' a fade for parts unknown."

"Short Change is not going anywhere," I said. "This is his territory. He's probably packing and ready to go toe to toe with Ozzie."

"Maybe. But then again, suppose it wasn't him. Suppose it was somebody else?"

"Like who?"

Bert shrugged and sighed. "Too soon to tell. But you know me. I keeps my ear open."

I retrieved Ruffin from the parking meter and walked east on 135th Street toward Malcolm X Boulevard. The floodlit basketball court adjoining the Harlem YMCA was filled with the whoop and yell of young men choreographing lickety-split moves, dribbling, dodging, feinting at an opening, then charging with the ball free and fast down the asphalt for the layup.

The shouting drifted on the wind as I walked past the gray-marbled facade of Harlem Hospital, where I had recently started my new job. I knew I could live comfortably on my impending settlement but I needed to put my MSW degree to use. The hospital was ideal because I could walk to work, interact with the community, and make myself generally useful. In the social work department I was assigned three days a week to the support group for AIDS patients.

Dad was ecstatic, Tad was happy, Elizabeth Jackson, my long-time friend and attorney, was relieved. I was doing what I should have been doing the day my diploma hit the palm of my hand. Instead I had opted for the NYPD, where meeting Tad was the only good thing that happened.

Near Lenox Terrace, I peeked in the window of Twenty-Two West, the neighborhood bar, but with Ruffin in tow, I couldn't step in, nor could I tie him to another parking meter. He was a patient dog but he had his limits, so I retraced my steps, threading my way through the sunglass, umbrella, and T-shirt vendors in front of Pan Pan's restaurant. I wandered through this brisk commerce and wondered if any of the vendors realized they were operating in the tradition of "Pig Foot Mary," a woman who once peddled boiled pigs' feet next to a newsstand on this very site in the '30s. Dad said that she then parlayed her nickels into brick and mortar and eventually acquired enough real estate to make her a very wealthy woman.

Strains of Randy Crawford's "*Wishing on a Star*" drifting from downstairs let me know Dad was home. I poked my head in the door leading down to his studio. "How's Ozzie?"

Dad, looking as if he hadn't slept in a month, came up the stairs. "Not too good. I'm going back in a little while. Want to come?"

"Why not," I said, wondering what else I could do besides

maybe fix a hot meal for them. I was sure neither had eaten in the last twenty-four hours.

Seventeen blocks to Ozzie's place wasn't that far and I could've covered the distance in a few minutes, but I matched my pace with Dad, who walked so slow, I thought he was inspecting for potholes. His head was down, making it hard for me to read his face. I wondered if the slowdown was brought on by fatigue or the thought of what awaited him when he saw Ozzie again.

Grief drains everything except rage and the unscratchable itch for revenge. I knew how Ozzie felt and I knew that Dad had absorbed his anger and the fearful realization that it could've been me. He had already lost my sister, Benin, to an accident in Europe, and so Ozzie's pain became his, reopening a door he had fought hard to close.

Not until we'd strolled for several blocks and passed the Unity Funeral Home on 126th Street, where a small crowd was gathered, did Dad look up and draw a deep breath. "I have to watch my man, keep tabs on him for the next couple of weeks. He thinks that pimp did it. That Short Change got to Starr because she had testified against him when he was busted on that drug deal."

"Why would he kill her?" I said. "He didn't do that much time, considering the weight he'd been caught with."

"I know. Folks in the know are saying he cut a deal, gave up some names. So they weren't surprised to see him back on the street two weeks ago. Even though rumor had it that he was good for at least twenty years.

"He was into a lot of things. Drugs. Prostitution. And when

he pulled Starr into it, Ozzie whipped his butt so bad, it was a miracle he survived. Ozzie can't go that way again. If he does, he's gotta go with correct stuff."

I glanced at Dad, suddenly afraid for him as well as for his friend. "Can't you talk him out of it?"

The only answer I heard was a hard grunt.

At 125th Street, we turned west and made our way through the evening crowd emerging from the subway at St. Nicholas Avenue. We passed the old Sydenham Hospital, closed years ago amid intense community opposition. Edward I. Koch, the mayor at the time, who'd spent most of his energy asking "How'm I doin'?" had added fuel to the fire of protest by donning an Afro wig at a political function and commenting, "Why do I hear the sounds of hospitals closing?" The photo, and the statement, had propelled thousands of people into the streets in outrage. Barricades had been thrown up. Mounted police patrolled. Dr. Eugene Callender led the full choir from the Church of the Master on Morningside Avenue and joined the crowd where they circled the hospital and prayed. The days that followed saw several arrests but in the end, the Wigged One prevailed, the institution was closed, and the patients were shifted elsewhere. After the bedlam subsided, the facility was modernized and converted into a residence for seniors; however, even today I cannot pass the gracious exterior and tranquil garden without all these memories getting in the way.

On Manhattan Avenue, some of the subway crowd stepped into the soft and elegant interior of Perk's Restaurant. For a brief second, I thought of trying to pull Dad and Ozzie out of the house for dinner but tonight was not the time. What was needed at the moment was what Mom used to call "wake and worry" food. Eat all you can at the wake and worry about your weight later.

Wake food, she had said, was down-home heavy, with enough fat and calories to drown the deepest sorrow and heavy enough to have you back on your feet in no time. Not necessarily smiling, but back on your feet where you belonged.

I missed Mom. And her cooking. The nearest thing to it and the most practical option under the circumstances was to call Charleston for a delivery.

At Ozzie's door, Dad produced a key. "If he's asleep, this way we won't disturb him. We'll just sit 'til he wakes. The shape he's in, he'll be glad to see someone when he opens his eyes."

We entered the wide foyer and our footsteps echoed across the oak floor. Then I felt silence close in like a veil. Off the foyer to the left was a large room dominated by a Steinway grand facing the window. The window was large and bare of curtains and I could see a tree outside, thick and green, and I imagined Ozzie sitting here with the sun's rays slanting across his broad shoulders.

We found him slouched at the small bar in the living room, a half-empty quart bottle of Absolut and an empty orange juice carton at his elbow. His eyes, when he focused on us, were like warning lights stuck on red. I expected Dad to move the bottle but he surprised me by bringing two more glasses from behind the bar and filling them half full. He handed one to me. One drink later, Dad spoke. "How you doin', man? You get any sleep?" He waited for an answer and got none.

"Listen, Ozzie. There's stuff I need to know before I can get started."

"Like what?" Ozzie glanced at him, then shifted his gaze toward the window. "Started on what?"

Rage lay just beneath the surface and I held my breath, hoping Dad would tread carefully.

"Like, you know, where you keep your papers, insurance, things like that. I need to call the—"

"I got just the thing for him," Ozzie said softly, as if Dad had not spoken. He raised his glass to his mouth. He still had not spoken to me. I wondered if he'd even seen me.

"What thing?" Dad whispered. "For whom?"

"Short Change. I got on the horn after you left and I found out where he's hangin'."

I saw Dad's shoulders fall. He looked at his friend leaning on the bar, staring at whatever folks stare at when life knocks them to the edge.

"Ozzie, wait a minute. Wait. Let's do one thing at a time. You can always catch up with Short Change, you know. Right now we have to think about putting Starr to rest. We gotta do that, okay?"

Dad spoke just above a whisper, trying to diffuse the pressure that lay just below the skin of this man built like he could've probably taken on Ali in his heyday. I looked at the muscled arms and thick neck and at the contradiction of his slender fingers that could move like a whisper over the keys.

I left Dad talking and walked into the kitchen, a large room with a beamed ceiling and exposed brick walls. A center island inlaid with rose-veined marble was crowded with high-tech appliances but the fridge was bare except for a jar of vitamins, more orange juice, a container of tofu that was frozen solid, and trays of ice cubes. Of course he hadn't had time to shop since he'd been back. Neither had we.

I dialed Charleston's, explained the situation, and ordered enough food to last at least two days. Back in the living room, Dad was not having much luck. I hoped the food would help.

A half hour later, Jo Jo, Charleston's delivery man, placed three large brown boxes on the table in the foyer and waved away the twenty I held out to him.

"Charleston said don't worry about it. Said he's sorry about your loss."

"That's very thoughtful," I said, pulling a five from another pocket. Jo Jo backed away, his fingers locked almost in prayer. "Nope. No tip on this trip, Sister Mali. I'm sorry too about your loss."

He headed down the steps, adjusted the car-sized headlight on the bike's handle bars, and glided silently away.

I had eaten so much at Bert's, I was no longer hungry but Dad and Ozzie—once I opened the cartons and the aroma hit them—had no problem putting away the offering. Ozzie seemed calmer now, and appeared to listen as Dad spoke. I breathed a sigh, unsure if it was relief or something else. I put the leftovers in the fridge and returned to the living room, where Dad had Ozzie's phone book and was already making calls. Ozzie leaned back on the sofa, eyes closed, and I wondered if he was listening or had simply drifted away again.

Dad nodded toward me. "You may as well go on home. Keep Ruffin company. I'll be here awhile. Probably all night."

He tapped the pages of the small book propped open before him.

"A lot of calls."

Ozzie opened his eyes and waved his hand wordlessly as I started for the door.

I crawled into bed and darkness closed around me immediately.

The Yacht Club Lounge on the upper deck was crowded for the midnight jam session and I sat ringside watching the musicians set up. The ocean was so smooth, my champagne glass rested without a tremor on the small table before me. Christian McBride and Stanley Turrentine strolled in, waved, and took a seat near Ivan Dixon, the actor.

Ozzie leaned over the piano and Dad and two other musicians stood next to him in the small halo of light. Ozzie ran his thumb down the keys as Dad parted his mouth in a quiet laugh at a private joke. Then the horn men cut in and red and blue lights glinted off the trombones as Al Grey and Mike Grey got down to business in a duet of "Autumn Leaves."

I tapped my feet, then felt a light tap on my shoulder. Tad was leaning next to me. His soft voice seemed to float through the music.

"I was looking all over for you, baby. Come back to the cabin. I want to show you something."

The something turned out to be him, which was all right with me. The cabin was quiet except for the light thrum of the engine. It was close and very dark and I'd barely had time to slip out of my dress before he was beside me, then on me in a strong, urgent instant, then softly kissing the thigh that I had complained about, easing up to my stomach, my breasts, the ribs under my breasts.

I felt his mouth draw tight against my skin. And suddenly, suddenly, there was a noise, this damn noise intruding. And Tad seemed to float out of my arms to the door. He stepped into the corridor and disappeared but not before I glimpsed a woman who was wearing even less than I was. And I couldn't move. I struggled but something held me to the bed.

The shock of the phone jolted me. I sat straight up, disoriented, bracing against the rolling of the water except there was no water. I was home and in my own bed. The ringing continued and

I pressed the speaker button. Dad's voice was tight with panic: "Mali. I just woke up."

"So did I," I murmured. My chest was still pounding from the dream. I glanced at the clock, which read 3 A.M.

"Dad? What happened?"

He hesitated, then said, "Ozzie's not here, Mali. He's cut out."

I was sitting in the living room trying to figure out the meaning of the dream when I heard the key in the door. Dad sank onto the sofa and passed his hands over his eyes. "Damn. I haven't felt this worn out in years."

The changes in his face frightened me. He was beginning to look like a different person, a tired stranger.

"Dad. I know how you feel about Ozzie, but you won't be able to help him if you fall out from exhaustion."

"Yeah. But—he's out there somewhere. Lookin' for—"

"Looking for trouble," I said as I rose to fix him a cup of coffee. "Listen, I'll speak to Tad, let him take it from here."

He also rose from the sofa and began to pace the floor. "Look, Mali. All due respect to Tad and all that, but what are the cops gonna do? It's not a kidnap or a disappearance. A man, a grown man, has simply walked out of his house. He's not disoriented, not on medication. Plus, he's black. You know the deal. You think the cops are gonna care? The only time they look for a black person is for target practice, to pump him with forty-one bullets!"

What could I say? I thought of Diallo, Glover, Cedeno, Huang, Baez, Rosario, Bumpers. Victims of police brutality and part of a list so long, it sickened me to think about it. Dad was right and he was wrung out, drained from anger, fatigue, and frustration. I poured the coffee and in a matter of minutes he was calm enough to slide into a light sleep. I sat in the chair across from him, watching, listening in the silence to the small sounds he made, listening also for that other sound, a quiet familiar voice that always seemed to come when I needed it:

"Girl, if you want something done and done right, you have to do it yourself. Didn't I teach you anything?"

"Yes, Mama. You taught me a lot."

"Hunh?" Dad had turned over on the sofa and was staring at me. "You say something?"

"Yes. I think you should go to bed."

I couldn't wait for what polite folks considered a decent hour before disturbing anyone with a phone call, but Tad was awake and must have been expecting me because he picked up on the first ring. Before I could tell him about Ozzie, he said, "I spoke to the lab techs. Most of the prints lifted off the switchplate, the side of the door, several drinking glasses, and the phone in Starr's bedroom, were put through the computer. We have a lot of interesting stuff."

He hesitated and I waited, wondering what was coming.

"We lifted prints from several people but Henry Stovall's, a.k.a. Short Change's, and Travis Morgan's are spread out like a road map."

"Travis Morgan?"

"Yep. He applied for a gun permit several years ago when he opened his business. Prints are on file. And you know Short Change's prints are filed."

I closed my eyes. Travis Morgan? Did Ozzie know something he hadn't mentioned to Dad? What was going on?

"Ozzie thinks Short Change might have done it," I said. "He's on the street now, looking for him."

"Ozzie? What's happening with him?"

"He's disappeared. Dad fell asleep at his place and woke up to find that he had cut out. Ozzie had said he had something for Short Change."

Tad cut me off, probably because he heard the rise in my voice. "Now look, Mali. Don't. Do not get involved. I know you. Ready to poke your head in something that—"

"Tell me," I said, "will the police look for him?"

Tad's silence lasted less than a second. "Don't confuse the issue. I'm asking you personally not to get involved. I'll do what I can."

He hung up and I sat on the edge of my bed, wide awake now.

"I'll do what I can." That's what doctors say when they're not sure if they're able to save a patient. "I'll do what I can."

I must have dozed off again but woke up determined not to become obsessed by that earlier stupid dream. Dad was out walking Ruffin so I showered, skipped breakfast except for a quick cup of coffee, and slipped into my favorite "Million Woman March" T-shirt and a pair of jeans.

It was still early and I wanted to hit the bricks before Tad had a chance to detour me. Bert hadn't gotten as much news as I had anticipated, probably because her circumstances had changed—Franklin was her focus now, not the puzzle and mystery of other people's lives. Or maybe the news was slow coming in. I don't know. I'd check back with her later, but meanwhile Miss Viv at the Pink Fingernail seemed a good bet.

Viv had worked briefly in Bert's shop a few summers ago. Bert had offered her refuge of sorts and a place to work after she had been dealt a low blow by her boyfriend, Johnny Harding, the biggest drug dealer uptown who also had connections with the precinct.

After some tricky maneuvers, Viv had not only regained her beauty shop, which Johnny had cheated her out of, but when the smoke cleared she was able to view her ex laid out in the cheapest cardboard casket ever stapled together. Of course she had had a little help and had never forgotten the favor.

On 140th Street, I walked past the Mahalia Jackson school and St. James Church and up the steep hill near the edge of St. Nicholas Park, where a squad of teenagers already had a basketball game going.

At Amsterdam Avenue a few doors past the soul food restaurant, which was closed, and the check-cashing business, which was open, the rose-tinted entrance of the Pink Fingernail Salon glowed like a beacon. It was a few minutes past nine on Wednesday, a midweek morning, and the salon's seven operators were already booked and several other women sat in the pink leather lounge chairs, waiting when I walked in. The sister at the station nearest the door smiled.

"You Viv's friend, right? I recognize those beautiful eyes. She's in the other shop, the barber's. Have some coffee, she'll be right back."

I maneuvered through the waiting group to a small table in the rear of the shop and helped myself to a jelly doughnut and a half cup of coffee. Then I found a seat and allowed myself to drift a little to the sound of the Temptations flowing from the small wall-mounted speakers. "Some Enchanted Evening" was an old, old song but bumped with a whole new rhythm.

The rhythm of the Temps wrapped around me as easily as a man's arms and I nearly convinced myself that it would be all right to stay all day. I was reaching for a fat pecan bun covered with icing when the door connecting the barber shop opened behind me.

Miss Viv let out a cry of surprise. "Girl! How you doin'?" She embraced me, then held me at arm's length. "You lookin' pretty as ever. Your skin is glowing. Life must be good indeed."

"I'm doing fine, Viv. And I see you are too. This place is probably the busiest uptown. Not a vacant seat in sight."

"Well, Mali, busy or not, you know I'm always glad when you drop in. I make the time for you, girl. As a matter of fact, I was gonna call you—"

"Now, Viv . . ."

"Honest. I was." She stepped away from me and I studied her. Her beautiful face was framed by the cascade of braids with pale auburn strands woven in and she had not lost a pound and didn't intend to. Once she had recovered from Johnny Harding, she had learned to love herself just the way she was. But now, a shadow passed over her face and her brow was wrinkled.

"What is it, Viv? Are you all right? What were you gonna call me about?"

She looked around and shrugged. "Well, maybe it ain't that bad. Maybe you already know."

She waved her hand, signaling me to follow her through the narrow entrance into the barber shop. The sound of the Temps faded as she closed the door and we stood in the center of the room, where chrome-accented fixtures and the row of black leather chairs on the terrazzo floor contrasted sharply with the soft pink next door. The shop was just opening for the day and the interior was cool and still empty except for one of the three female barbers who sat in a chair near the back, reading.

Viv and I moved to stand near the front entrance and Viv spoke softly so as not to disturb her.

"Were you on the *QE2* last week?"

I looked at her, marveling at how fast news traveled. "Yes, I was."

"Were you asleep?"

"We all have to sleep sometimes," I said, wondering what her point was.

"Just checking. I was gonna call you tonight and pull your coat."

"About what?"

"About a customer of mine. I was gonna let you know that a Chrissie Morgan—she's a regular—but you're my friend... Anyway, she was in here yesterday getting her hair together and talkin' about the cruise and about how a certain real fine-lookin' brother named Honeywell was all in her grille from the time she stepped on deck. Couldn't leave her in peace, and all that."

I felt a tight band clamp on the side of my jaw; I heard a grinding noise almost like a jackhammer and realized it was my teeth. If Miss Chrissie had walked into the shop just then, she wouldn't have had to worry ever again about getting her hair cut, dyed, bleached, or fried. I would've taken care of every damn strand.

Miss Viv continued, ignoring my silence. "She said that he was payin' close attention, particular attention to her."

Close attention. Particular attention. Chrissie had the story all wrong, had it the other way around.

I remembered Tad and I leaning at the rail port side on the upper deck, the sun sinking fast because there was nothing in its way.

The sky at the flat edge of the horizon had turned pink, purple, then gray, and then you blinked and it was dark.

New York's skyline had long vanished and we were heading for Bar Harbor. The moon had risen now and the dark waves sparkled as if someone had flung a handful of diamonds overboard.

Tad rubbed his shoulder against mine, then traced his finger along the nape of my neck. "I'm going to try my luck at the slots again. Want to come?"

We could hear the faint clamor of the casino bells but I nodded. "No. I'll stay here. Just because you won big an hour ago doesn't mean you'll be lucky again."

"Won big? You call five hundred dollars big?"

"Yes, I do, if you manage to hang on to it, but you seem anxious to give it right back."

"Ah, Mali. Even if I do, I'm giving back their own dollars. I'll stop at two hundred and still come out ahead. See you in an hour."

He kissed me and made his way past the Crystal Bar and into the casino.

I remained where I was for a few minutes, then wandered downstairs to the quarterdeck to browse through the library and bookstore. Minutes later, I wandered toward the elevator, wondering if Tad was winning or losing. If he had lost, he'd be back at the rail again. I returned to the upper deck but the spot where he'd left me was occupied by a young Asian couple, holding hands and alternately gazing at the stars and then at each other.

I eased into a lounge chair and watched them, hoping they'd move on, stroll down the deck or something. I regarded this as my favorite spot and now it was unavailable.

I finally abandoned my chair and walked toward the sound of the ringing bells. Maybe Tad was pushing the right lever again, turning the one-armed bandit into a cash cow. I entered the casino and found him seated at the end of a row of clanging, light-changing, money-hungry machines and totally absorbed in feeding one coin after another into the slot.

And I saw that Chrissie Morgan was totally absorbed in him. She leaned over his shoulder so close, if she had hiccuped, her boobs would have spilled out of the low-cut sweater she had stuffed herself into, an iridescent-yellow crochet number more suitable for a younger, less developed woman.

I heard her coo and cluck above the bells, "Oh. Oh, Tad! You're so good, you're so—"

I listened to the sounds, wondering if she were about to experience an orgasm. When I tapped her shoulder, she looked up with a bright smile and whispered, "Hope you don't change his luck. He's doing so well."

Then she patted his shoulder the way one would pat a dear, familiar friend. "Must run. Show's about to start."

I watched her walk down the narrow aisle past the dice table and the teller's window and melt into the crowded corridor. Then I turned to Tad, who had risen from the small stool in front of the machine. The tray was filled with silver coins, as were four plastic quart-size tubs on either side.

I said nothing. He shrugged and spread his hands, palms up, as if to say, "What was I supposed to do? I can't keep her out of here."

My expession was wordless and from the look on his face, he must have understood my anger. He stepped toward me. "Now look, Mali. I—"

Just then, someone must have hit a superjackpot because the machine at the other end of the aisle lit up extra bright and the clanging was so loud, it sounded like a major fire alarm. Heads turned, folks gathered, and two attendants wearing bright professional smiles glided over bearing a tray of the quart-size plastic tubs plus containers the size of Mickey Dee's large-size Cokes.

There was plenty of excitement and I turned and left him standing in it.

Outside, the Asian couple had moved on and my favorite spot was once again available but my mood had changed. I neither saw nor cared what the moon looked like now. I walked along the port side until the mist bathing my skin cooled me enough to think rationally. Then I went down to the number-two deck to the purser's office near the midship's lobby to get Chrissie's phone number. That girl and I needed to talk, and fast.

When I dialed, there was no answer. I'd catch up with her eventually, probably at breakfast tomorrow morning.

I needed to go back to the cabin and shower and get ready for Dad's show. And also to turn off the scene playing hardball in my head. I slipped the key in the lock and Tad was inside, slouched in the chair, his long legs stretched nearly to the bed and his head resting against the wall.

I closed the door behind me and leaned against it, waiting, although I didn't exactly know what I was waiting for.

Finally, he rose and stepped toward me. "Look, baby, I'm sorry. I—"

"You have nothing to be sorry about," I said. "I intend to have a talk with her and that should—"

"Mali, please. I know your temper. When you get angry..."

I was against the door and there was nowhere to move. He was crowding me and I needed space. Space to think. But that didn't happen. His hands were on my shoulders and sliding down to my waist, then up again to the small of my back. And his voice was softer than usual.

"Mali, baby. Don't do this. This trip was supposed to be something special for us. Don't. Don't. I love you. We've been through too much, baby. I love you."

I rested my head on his shoulder and we made our way in small steps toward the bed and sat on the edge. "I'm not really angry with you," I said. "I'm upset with Chrissie. She's on you like a bee on honey and doesn't care who knows it. I have to talk to her. I don't like it and I intend to let her know."

"Can't it wait?"

"For what?"

"For this," he whispered, easing the zipper down the back of my dress and taking it off, then fingering the hooks in my bra. "Can't it wait, baby?"

"I don't know," I whispered. "Convince me. Try real hard."

And that was the real deal. Now I was standing here listening to Miss Viv spin this fantasy.

She glanced at me, saw my expression, and quickly added, "Of course I know Chrissie can stretch stuff. Ain't no shame to her game. But she ain't mentioned the problem she havin' tryin' to keep her own man in check."

"Really?" I managed to say.

"That's right. Travis had a thing for that girl that just got killed. That Starr Hendrix."

Now I was really interested. "You don't say."

"Yep. Miss Chrissie never mentioned that, as long as she been comin' here. Never talked about that and it had been goin' on for a while. One of my operators told me. So when she came with that tale about your honey, I figured she was either fishin', wishin', fantasizin', or just plain lyin'. Either which way, I thought you ought to know. So you could pay close attention."

Close attention. Yes, indeed. With my size-ten sneaker in her butt when I catch up with her. But first, I'd whip her for lying and whip her again for trying.

Miss Viv looked in my face and read my mind. "Listen, Mali. I'm tellin' you this 'cause of what you did for me when I went through that bad time. But don't let this get you. Ain't no contest when the girl got to take off half a pound of makeup, half her hair, both eyes, and a Wonderbra before she can jump in the sack to do the do. By the time she get ready, the brother probably so tired, he zone out. Now I see you frownin', Mali, but you straighten out that face. Bottom line is Miss Thing can't touch your program."

Miss Viv talked straighter than Miss Bert and had a knack for adding a word or two of comfort. My jaw slackened and the pressure squeezing the air out of my chest eased up. I was no longer ready for combat but ready for more information. Tad had said Travis Morgan's prints as well as Short Change's prints were in Starr's apartment.

"Starr was seeing Travis Morgan? I thought she'd been hooked up with Short Change."

Miss Viv slowly whirled one of the barber's chairs around and took a seat. Then she pointed toward the other, motioning me to sit down. "Lemme tell you," she said. "That Short Change was somethin' else. He—"

"What do you mean, was?"

She leaned back in the chair as if I had pushed her. "You ain't heard the word?"

Here we go again, I thought. Can't close your eyes for one second in Harlem without something jumping off. "No, I haven't heard a thing."

"They found 'im early this morning. Somebody opened a third eye in the middle of his forehead. Left him on the sidewalk and the thirty-eight in the gutter."

I was glad I was sitting down. My head filled with thoughts of Ozzie and suddenly I felt afraid for him. Where was he? Did he do this? I should've kept my mouth shut. Not told Tad a thing. Now every precinct in Harlem would be out to get him. I needed to get home. Talk to Dad.

"Maybe it was suicide," I said when I'd gotten my thoughts back on track.

Miss Viv shook her head emphatically, her braids moving in a multicolored swirl around her face. "No way. Street had it that he was one of them good-doin' players. No good-doin' pimp gonna do the suicide thing. Shit like that blow a hole in the code. Short Change had six workin' girls pullin' big dollars. He had one for every day of the week but Sunday."

"Which one was Starr?"

"Wednesday. She was supposed to be his Wednesday woman, but she didn't last but a minute before she quit."

"Why'd she quit?"

Miss Viv shrugged. "Can't tell what I don't know. I do know she had started dippin' and dabbin' and you know the deal. Ain't nobody I know can outplay the White Lady. Heroin'll beat you up, knock you down, and have you crawlin' sideways like a crippled crab."

Miss Viv rose from the chair. "Starr was a cute kid. Too bad that snake got a hold of her."

One of the operators from the salon opened the door. "Sorry to interrupt, but your ten o'clock is here."

"Be right there," Viv said and turned to me again. "Maybe we can sit down over dinner sometime at Wells. Their fried chicken is the best thing goin'."

"So is the peach cobbler," I said. "It's a deal. Just let me know."

I stepped from the shop into the still-cool morning and made my way down the hill again. This time I moved quickly, wondering what I was going to tell Dad. I cut through Bradhurst Avenue at 145th Street and back again to Eighth Avenue at 140th Street past the St. Charles townhouses.

When I reached home my mind was still fixed on Short Change and how he'd died.

Dad opened the door before I put my key in the lock.

"Any word from Ozzie?" I asked.

"Not a note. I've called, left messages. I don't know."

I looked at his face and knew he hadn't heard the latest news. "Dad, we have to find him before the cops do."

My father had started toward the kitchen and turned back, his eyes narrowed. "Why? What's happened?"

"I just left the Pink Fingernail. Viv's place. She said Short Change was found dead. Shot."

My father leaned against the wall and I saw him hold his hand to his chest as if to keep something from falling out. He blinked rapidly and I barely heard him whisper, "This is my fault. I fell asleep and he slipped out."

I led him back to the living room and he sank—collapsed was a better word—into a chair. I hurried to the kitchen and returned with a cup of coffee. "We don't know if Ozzie did this. Could've been anyone," I said, trying to convince myself as well. "People in that life have a lot of enemies. Have to watch their back twenty-four seven. We don't know yet who did it."

"And neither does that so-called street crime unit," Dad snapped. "They'll use up a load of dumdum bullets and then all the marches and protests in the world won't bring him back!"

I said nothing. I was the one who'd told Tad about Ozzie. I had opened my big mouth and said that Ozzie had gone looking for Short Change. Gone looking with blood in his eye. I had to find him before the cops did.

8

I placed the phone on the table near the sofa and persuaded Dad to lie down. Then I went upstairs and changed into linen slacks and a silk jacket. When I came downstairs again, he was staring at the ceiling as if contemplating the designs on the crown molding, but I knew better. He was thinking of Ozzie.

"I'll be back in a few hours, Dad. You're too stressed to do anything else so try to get some sleep. If Tad calls, tell him I went to the movies or something. Better yet, let the machine kick in. Don't answer unless it's Ozzie."

I stuffed my notebook into my shoulder bag,

grabbed my straw hat, and left the house. It was going on high noon as I hurried toward Powell Boulevard but a bit too early to pick up the details I needed because most of the night people were still in a coma. The bars were not yet open and if they were, I'd have to be careful. I did not want under any circumstance to run into Tad.

On Powell Boulevard I turned into 134th Street, where I passed a convoy of old cars, large as boats, that would have been considered classics in more well-to-do neighborhoods. They were docked curbside bumper to bumper with windows down and doors open wide to accommodate drop-ins. Men, older and more damaged than the cars they had sought refuge in, shuttled brown-bagged bottles from the front seat to the rear and back again. They were strangers to life's promises, only dimly aware of Wall Street with its frenzied optimism and wild profits. "The Street" was foreign territory to which they had no passport. Dow Jones might have been the name of a distant planet. So the brown bags helped to negotiate a tenuous sort of peace with their reality and they took time out to greet me pleasantly as I walked by.

I waved back, balanced not by memory but by the history of other lives lived large just blocks away. I knew that in the back of memory, at least a few of these men also remembered when Erroll Garner, Buck Clayton, Don Byas, Dizzy Gillespie and his wife, and Billy Eckstine and his wife had, at one time or another, lived in the same apartment building at 2040 Seventh Avenue, just a few blocks away. And they had hung out in Sugar Ray's, Small's Paradise, Jock's Place, the Red Rooster, Connie's Inn, the Club Baron, Shalimar's, Basie's Lounge, and the other bars and clubs long before the avenue was called Powell Boulevard.

I did not look back at the men in the cars but continued to walk, thankful to Dad for telling me this stuff. It'll keep me balanced, he'd said.

I reached Malcolm X Boulevard and some other things began to fall in place. Today was Wednesday and something had to be done fast. I wasn't concerned about Ozzie missing Dad's next gig. Dad could always get another piano man. That was no problem. The main thing was to ensure that Ozzie remained alive, even if he never played another note.

I walked the few blocks to Charleston's Bar-Be-Que restaurant, although calling his sliver of a place a restaurant was stretching it a bit. It was really a take-out restaurant with the barbecuing done outdoors.

At curbside in front of the store, the converted oil drums which served as cookers were not yet fired up. The grills as usual had been scrubbed the night before and now Charleston was inside, bleaching the narrow counters and other work surfaces. Jo Jo, clad in a rubber apron that dwarfed his thin frame, had just finished washing the tiled walls with a long-handled brush.

I knocked on the window and Charleston smiled, glad to see me. Jo Jo smiled also, glad for a break. The shop was so narrow that he prepared to step out to allow me to step in.

"Don't go too far," Charleston warned. "We still got work to do. Got to get those stoves up and running."

Jo Jo looked at him from the door, then glanced down at his water-logged outfit and heavy gloves. "Where am I gonna go in this getup?"

"How should I know? Downtown to the Plaza, maybe."

Jo Jo made a face as he leaned the brush against the counter then stepped out to prepare the stoves.

"He's a good kid," Charleston said as he turned from the window. "Boy was in eight foster homes 'til he aged out at eighteen. Can you beat that? That's how the state spends your tax money. Warehouse 'em. No trainin'. Kids in school doin' classwork in the damn bathroom, so schools ain't worth shit. So no education. And next stop naturally is upstate and into the system all over again. This time maybe for ten, twenty years."

"The prison industrial complex is big big business," I said.

"Prison industrial bullshit," Charleston snapped, scrubbing the counter harder. "It's a new name for an old game: slavery. I was in it, remember? So I'm a' try to see that Jo Jo don't end up in it."

"What happened to his folks?"

"Who knows? He don't even know. Anyway, he's a good kid. Bad breaks just happened, that's it. He was livin' in a basement without runnin' water and hangin' outside beggin' for enough coins to keep skin and bone together, to get himself somethin' to eat. Now he gets a salary and he makes enough just from the tips alone to rent a little kitchenette, buy some decent clothes, and think beyond where his next meal is comin' from. He's writin' rap poetry, thinkin' about becomin' a star."

I stood near the soapy counter as Charleston continued to clean it. Watching him with his huge bulk and scowling face, you'd think he was the meanest man in the world, then he'd smile and you'd know better.

"So what's up with you, Mali? Guess you heard the word on Short Change."

"Yep. Fast track slowed him down."

Charleston nodded. "Wonder what his ladies gonna do?"

I looked out of the window, feeling the two inches of hair on my head rise in irritation. I wanted to say or at least theorize that the ladies might possibly think about going out on their own. Booker T. and Garvey and Elijah had all preached "doing for self" even if they didn't have these particular occupations in mind. But so what? Why shouldn't these women do for themselves? Why turn over their hard-earned—and they were hard-earned—dollars to a pimp?

If I opened this line of conversation, I'd probably be here all day arguing and Charleston had work to do. He needed to be ready when the folks started lining up outside and I needed any lead that would keep me one step ahead of the cops. So I said, "Were Short Change's women from around the neighborhood?"

"Yep."

"You delivered?"

"All the time. Folks like my secret sauce and they was no exception."

"Same address?"

"Naw. S.C. had 'em spread out. That way they don't get in no cat fights over him. He make his rounds, pick up the dollars, and drop a little something to keep 'em all happy."

I nodded, easing farther into the tight space to rest my elbows on the bit of counter that was dry.

"Charleston, you know what I need?"

He paused to look at me. "Damn, Mali. Why?"

"No. No. I don't need the lock picks. I'm not planning to sneak into anybody's apartment."

"I hope not. Last time, you was just plain lucky. Now you dealin' with a different crew. If one of these sisters catch you, they jack you up so high, your feet won't touch the ground for a week."

I wondered how the sisters in question could be so self-reliant in some ways and so dependent in others. "All I want," I said, "are some addresses. I intend to ring the bells and walk in like a normal human being. If they let me."

"Why you need to see them?"

"Because I need some answers. Because Ozzie is Dad's friend and Dad's seriously affected by this. Now Ozzie's disappeared and there's talk that he might've gotten to S.C. because he thinks the pimp killed his daughter."

"Ozzie? Why would he think that?"

"Starr testified against S.C., remember?"

"Oh yeah." Charleston rubbed his face and left a thin streak of soap suds on his chin. "Well, I hope you tag 'im before that street unit git to him. They way outta hand now. Remember when they shot up that rapper, ODB, in Brooklyn on a hummer? Now they kill that African brother? This is some way-out shit. Was those cops cokin', smokin', or just plain went crazy at the sight of an unarmed black man? Forty-one shots.

"And then they turn around and announce they gonna use dumdum bullets. Dummies usin' dumdums is damn dangerous. Why they nab ODB on the coast for sportin' a vest? Shit, the way things is jumpin' off, I'm thinkin' about gettin' measured for one myself. Along with a matchin' bulletproof hat, socks, and ear muffs. And that's just for summer gear. When the death squad come callin', I'm a be ready for they funky ass."

He slapped a sponge on the counter and I waited patiently for him to cool down, as much as it was possible to do so under the circumstances.

I remembered how Tad had talked about the murder, and how furious the black officers at the precinct house felt. They were angry enough about Amadou Diallo and about the torture of Abner Louima to join the public in a demand for justice.

Several minutes slid by and I listened in silence to the hard opening and closing of the fridge and to Charleston's choice adjectives.

After a while, I reminded him why I'd dropped in.

"Mali. I oughta start chargin' you. In fact, if it was anybody else, I'd tell 'em to go to hell, but you—"

Then he remembered the holdup incident a few years ago that I'd walked in on, which had probably saved his life and his cash, and he said no more. He wiped his hands on the plaid towel hanging from his back pocket and pulled a large accordion file from under the counter. It was filled with receipts and a spiral notebook containing addresses, phone numbers, and proper names and nicknames of his customers.

"Listen," he said as he flipped through the worn pages. Some entries were blurred and grease-stained, but he knew the names and who he was searching for. "Once I give up this info, you on your own, understand? I don't know shit if it blows back at you."

"Charleston, you know me better than that."

He wrote three names, addresses, and phone numbers on a torn sheet of paper and handed it across the counter. I scooped it up before he could change his mind and I was out the door so fast, one would have thought I had stolen a choice rack of ribs. I waved to Jo Jo and kept walking.

I hurried over to St. Nicholas Park and found a seat on a bench in the shade between the mothers and toddlers and baby strollers and old chess players. I took out my notebook and thought about my next move. Charleston had given me only three names: Monday-Amanda Johnson; Tuesday-Jeanette Beavers; Thursday-Myrtle Thomas. Wednesday-Starr Hendrix was dead.

What happened to Friday and Saturday? Miss Viv said there was no Sunday. I wondered if the girls were allowed to rest that day, or were all the johns in church busily experiencing the cleansing wonders of the Holy Ghost?

I jotted down a few more notes, vague descriptions that Charleston had given me, next to their names and then left the bench. At Seventh Avenue, I walked downtown again passing Wells Restaurant, where one day soon Viv and I would have serious business with the chicken and waffles.

At 125th Street near the Apollo Theatre, I entered the lobby of a small building leading upstairs to the law office of Elizabeth

Jackson, my friend and attorney. Elizabeth tries hard—but often fails—to keep me on the straight and narrow.

Her door was closed and I could hear the murmur of voices inside. She was interviewing a client so I waited in the anteroom and took the time to review my plans again. An hour later, her door opened and she escorted a tall, rather good-looking man to the stairs.

I heard his voice, low but strong: "Thanks again, Miss Jackson. The sooner the better."

And her voice, measured and reassuring: "Mr. Morgan, you can rely on me."

I knew it was him. Knew that long-legged, pigeon-toed walk. But his shoulders. Usually so straight he could've been the poster boy for the "The Few. The Proud. The Marines." His shoulders now seemed to fold against his chest like the wings of an injured bird. Why was he here? Did he feel that the police suspected him? Had they questioned him yet?

When Elizabeth walked back into the office, I was out of my seat before she could say hello. "That's Travis Morgan," I said. "What's he doing here?"

She said nothing and I followed behind her so closely I nearly tripped up when she stopped short. She turned to face me.

"Mali, what would've happened if you had dropped in an hour later or two hours earlier?"

"Nothing," I said, knowing exactly what she was getting at.

"Nothing is right," she said, "so we'll leave it right there."

Of course I couldn't leave it and tried to rearrange my question but Elizabeth was the attorney and skilled herself at rearranging such things as questions, especially after an objection has been raised.

"You know as well as I that I can't discuss any of my clients' business," she sighed. She took the band from her head and shook her cascade of auburn-tinted locks loose, ready to change the subject, ready to relax.

"I'm sorry, Elizabeth. Won't happen again."

She smiled because we both knew it wasn't true.

"Okay, so tell me about the trip. And the great time you had with your honey. I'm all ears and envy. Sure wish I could've been there."

"Don't complain. I know some attorneys who might have to apply at Mickey Dee's if they don't get something soon."

She moved from her desk to put some files away. "I'm not really complaining. This is what I want to do. This is what my dad did. Anyway, let's hear about the trip. Who was on board? Who was at Newport?"

I went over each detail but omitted the Chrissie Morgan stuff since her husband had just left the office. God knows what that was about, but I didn't want to complicate things any further. So I told her about Ruth Brown, Slide Hampton, Cassandra Wilson, Aretha, Lou Rawls, Sir Roland Hannah, Dave Brubeck, Branford Marsalis, James Moody. And, of course, my dad.

"That sounds like a cruise to heaven," she said. "Maybe next year . . ." Her voice trailed off and I decided to change the subject. I knew she hadn't taken a vacation for two years and needed some relief.

"I dropped by because I need some forms," I said.

"What kind?"

"Last will and testament."

"Oh?" She leaned forward and folded her arms on the desk. "Last will? Planning on leaving us?"

"Not just yet," I said.

"Why do you need them? I thought you and your dad had completed all of that a few years ago."

Now it was my turn to get cagey. "We did."

The statement hung in the air and another minute passed before she said, "Okay, how many do you need?"

"Three, if you have them," I said. The bell outside the office rang and she glanced at her watch. "My two o'clock appointment," she said. She extended the forms and I rose from the chair. "Thanks. I'll call tomorrow. We can play catch-up."

The Monday woman, Amanda Johnson, lived in a five-story red-brick walk-up on West 140th Street between Seventh and Lenox avenues a few doors away from the old P.S. 139, the Frederick Douglass Jr. High School, where the poet Countee Cullen once taught. The building now houses a seniors' center. The small park on the corner of Lenox Avenue was crowded with serious chess players hunkered down over their boards, oblivious to the rumble and blare of passing traffic. Not far from them, under a circle of trees, women exchanged news, and a few feet away two teenagers tended baby strollers.

I glanced at the girls and caught snatches of conversation: precocious, fresh, and funny. I watched them handle the strollers and hoped that at least one of them was the baby-sitter, older sister, or any relative other than mother.

The stoop of Monday's house was nearly as crowded as the corner park, and a thin woman in a faded housedress looked up when I said "Pardon me." She said nothing but shaded her eyes against the sun and let a second pass before she decided to move an inch to the left. This created a narrow path that allowed me to edge up the steps, putting one foot directly in front of the other. None of the sixteen or so "doormen" moved either and I felt like a tightrope walker as I manuevered my way through them and walked up to the third floor. Despite the stoop group, the hallways were clean and well lit and the gray-painted walls were graffiti-free.

At the end of the corridor I rang the bell and waited, then pressed the buzzer again. I was turning to leave when the door opened slowly.

"Yes?"

"I'm looking for Amanda Johnson," I said.

The girl nodded. She was either the daughter of the woman I was looking for or Short Change should've been thrown under the jail for statutory rape.

"I'm Amanda," she said. She spoke slowly, as if she had just woken up. She could not have been more than sixteen, about five feet three and perhaps one hundred ten pounds and quite pretty. Her brown skin was fair enough to reveal a splash of freckles across her nose, and her medium-length hair was actually in braids. Pigtails. Plaited the way I remembered my mother used to braid mine. I looked at this girl and remembered how I once held the jar of hair oil and sat on the floor between my mother's knees.

At that moment I was glad that Short Change had been taken out. And I hoped it hadn't been a sudden ambush, but drawn out long enough for him to beg for, and reflect on, his worthless life.

"Can I help you?"

Her accent let me know that she hadn't too long ago stepped off the Greyhound from some small Midwestern place. Short Change must have picked her up before she had had a chance to rest her suitcase on New York pavement.

"Ah, yes, Miss Johnson? My name is Miss Anderson and I'm from the Community Life Insurance Company. I'm here about Starr Hendrix. May I come in?"

Her face clouded and I saw a trace of suspicion but she opened the door wider.

"Come on in. I suppose it's okay."

She stepped back from the door and led me into a small, two-room apartment. I was surprised at the layout. The building had been renovated and looked new on the outside but I hadn't known that the old five-and six-room apartments inside had been sliced and diced to accommodate more people in less space. No wonder the stoop was crowded. There was nowhere to turn around inside.

I followed her into the larger of the two rooms, which seemed to double as a bedroom-living room. The sofa on which I sat was piled with clothes at one end, as was the floor. A mound of shoes and plastic boots, badly in need of repair, lay in the corner near the wall and I saw a tiny table nearby that held several wigs and jars of makeup. A small television set rested on a folding chair near the table. On the wall above the table was the familiar pictorial quartet of Malcolm, Martin, John, and Bobby—framed in brass and arranged in a step fashion with Malcolm at the top.

She settled herself in a chair opposite me and folded her hands in her lap, waiting.

"This is a nice apartment, very cozy," I said, looking around.

"Thanks. I need to clean some things out, but I've been so busy. Now I suppose . . ." She glanced at me. "You said something about insurance?"

"Yes. Starr Hendrix listed you as one of her contingent beneficiaries and I need some information."

"What's contingent?"

"It means that you're the second name on the policy. If the first person dies, then the second one, the contingent person, becomes the beneficiary."

"Really? Starr did that for me?"

"Yes. But if the first person dies less than a year after the policy was taken out, then the policy is void. Also, if the first person commits suicide within that year, it's void."

I was talking fast and she closed her eyes, confused. Shit, I was confused myself. I had planned to use the old last will and testament hustle, counting on good old-fashioned greed to extract the information I needed, but discarded that tactic when I looked at the scene. Now I felt terrible winging it like this. I had expected an older woman, a less innocent one with whom I could come right to the point if the will and testament bait didn't work. I would have said to the sister straight up: Look, Starr was murdered. Mack Daddy was iced. I'm Starr's cousin/sister/mama/friend/aunt on her mama's brother's side. Pick one. And I'm trying to find out whodunit. Or something like that.

"What kind of beneficiary?" Monday asked again.

I was afraid that she was going to reach for a pencil and write it down this time, but she didn't, and I repeated the confusing statement about first and second beneficiaries and suicide in the first year and so forth without tripping myself up.

"So," I said, reaching for my notebook before she could digest this concoction any further. "I just need you to answer a few questions. How long had you known Starr Hendrix?"

"Let's see. I got in the city . . . let's see. I met her two years ago. When I first came here. And, you know, like when I met her, she was who I wanted to be, you know?"

"I can understand that," I said, pretending to scribble something important. "Starr was going to be a star. That's what her daddy said."

Monday's face lost some of its softness and the frown got deeper. "But nobody heard nuthin'. Don't know when the funeral is or nuthin' and I want to go."

She traced the narrow line between her braids with her finger, then wound the tip of the braid around her thumb.

"I wanted to go into show business. Henry said when I first met him that he could set me up, help me meet the right people, get me on stage at the Apollo, but that would be only the first step. He knew a lot of people in show business, he said. But first—"

"But what?"

"But first, I needed some really nice clothes, and a new hairdo, and backup money."

"What's backup money?"

"You know. Money for clubs, cabs, and restaurants where you could be seen by the right people. Stuff like that. He was saving my money so I could go to acting school. He was gonna be my manager, he said. He said soon as I made enough for actin' school, he could work on gettin' me seen by the right people. He knew a lot of people."

I glanced at the pile of shoes and boots in the corner and looked down at my notebook again. Short Change must have repeated this until it took on the resonance of a mantra. "When last did you see Starr or Henry Stovall?" I said.

Again she closed her eyes and the braid twisting slowed. "I saw Starr one night about two weeks ago. She was with a tall, kinda nice-lookin' brother who had that walk, you know. Kinda pigeon-toed step that said groovin' with him wouldn'a been no problem at all.

"Starr told him to walk on a little ways and she stopped and spoke to me. Told me to get out of what I was doin', that Henry was gaming me. Well, Henry drove by while she was talkin'—you should see the wheels he pushin'. Beautiful car. He keeps himself in the latest Cadillac."

She spoke as if Henry "Short Change" Stovall were still among the living and was expected to knock on the door any minute and invite her out. I wanted to ask how often she rode in that car and she seemed to read my mind.

"Every night when he drop me off? I felt so good, I wanted to stay in that fine leather seat forever. But he said what I was doin' was for the both of us and soon as he made the right contacts, I would stop."

She looked down at the floor and I didn't press her.

"Okay, just to confirm his last known address, I need—"

"Well, he had a small place near the park. Marcus Garvey Park. Said he was gonna move to somethin' bigger soon as he could, but now . . ."

"Did anything happen the night Starr spoke to you? Did Henry do anything?"

"Not to her, no, ma'am. One thing about Starr, she didn't take no mess from nobody."

"Really?"

"Uhm-hmm. She had her own plans, she said. Let him and everybody else know that she wasn't gonna be out on the . . . uh . . ."

"So Henry didn't say anything? Didn't do anything?" I asked softly.

A minute passed before Monday's tears came, and then they were like a cloudburst, loud and uncontrollable. I searched frantically in my bag for a fistful of tissues and leaned over to extend them to her.

"I'm sorry," I said. "I know this is painful."

"No, it ain't. The pain happened that night, when I got off work. He picked me up, I handed him the money, nearly a thousand dollars, and he said, 'You did good, baby,' and he kissed me. And then when we got here, he beat me. Beat me 'til I couldn't move, I was so sore."

"Why?"

" 'Cause he had warned me to stay away from Starr. Said she was bad for me and for his business. Said he was gonna fix her."

"How?"

"I never found out. Maybe he planned to git her back on the drugs again or something. Teach her a lesson, he said."

"What are you going to do now?" I asked, dreading the answer. Some women on the stroll, especially if they worked alone, made so much money some nights that eventually it became hard to quit and deal with the ordinary flow of dollars.

I watched Monday shrug and close her eyes again, as if she wanted to block out the future.

"How old are you?" I asked, still jotting in my notebook.

"Twenty-one."

"What's your date of birth?" I asked quickly.

"Uh . . ."

I waited patiently as she struggled to add the number of years to her actual date in order to come up with an approximation.

"Oh shit," she sighed. "I never was good at numbers. I'm seventeen."

Seventeen. That meant that Short Change had picked her up when she was fifteen.

"You ever thought of going back home?"

"Naw. Maybe for a visit. But not yet. I haven't done what I set out to do. For me, it's do or die."

I said nothing. Do or die. It'd probably been that way also for Starr, the Wednesday woman.

"Listen," I said, handing her one of Elizabeth Jackson's cards. "I want you to call this number today. Not tomorrow but today. She's real nice and can put you in touch with some people, some agencies, who can help you. I mean really help you."

"What about the insurance thing?"

"I don't know. Starr's policy is less than a year old," I said, wondering how far I could stretch this lie. "You're the contingent—the second beneficiary. We have to prove that the first beneficiary—Henry Stovall—didn't commit suicide or do something to cause his own death. And after all that, we have to sort through all of his relatives who might pop out of the woodwork to contest the policy. This might take some time."

This seemed to satisfy her, but before I closed the notebook, I said, "Can you put me in touch with Henry's other . . . friends?"

"You mean his girls? Are their names on the policy?"

"No. But I need to speak to them anyway. Any information about the way he died will be helpful."

She moved from the small chair and walked into the other room. I couldn't see directly into the room but it sounded as if she was pulling a small box from a shelf of some kind. She brought the box, made of heavy corrugated cardboard and large enough to hold several pairs of shoes, into the room and placed it on the floor between us.

"See," she said, taking the cover off. "Starr taught me this. Always pay yourself first. God, I'm gonna miss her."

I stared open-mouthed at the stacks of bills: hundreds, fifties, twenties, old and new, large and small portraits of Franklins, Grants, Jacksons, tied in neat rubber-banded bundles. This had been a very busy little girl, who was not in such bad shape after all. I glanced up to catch her smiling at my surprise and I wondered if she planned to call Elizabeth.

"Here are some addresses, but one—Sara Lee Brown—I don't have 'cause she moved. Got evicted from her place."

I looked at the list. Two of the names I had already gotten from Charleston, so Sara Lee Brown and Martha Golden were the weekend women and Sara Lee was missing.

"When was Sara Lee evicted?"

"At least six months back. I don't know where she is now. You know, you kinda lose touch . . ."

"What does she look like?"

"Oh, about five-seven, pretty, with dark brown complexion, one hundred twenty pounds, about thirty-five years old, wore lots of blond wigs, 'cause blond hair catch the headlights, you know, especially in winter. It stand out real catchy when snow is fallin'."

10

I left Monday's apartment, not at all sure that she'd contact Elizabeth. I could have referred her to the social work department at the hospital but she was not sick. Stressed but not seriously ill. Besides, if she showed up on one of the days I was scheduled to work, it might cause a problem. Better to have her speak to Elizabeth.

I maneuvered once more through the gatekeepers, who had not budged an inch to the left or the right since my earlier entrance.

The block was also crowded with volleyball players, hopscotchers, and potential hoop stars. I threaded my way around the kids and at

Powell Boulevard decided to return home. I needed to see how Dad was feeling before continuing my rounds. Perhaps he'd heard from Ozzie.

I passed Mickey Dee's, crossed the boulevard, and turned into the relative stillness of Strivers Row. When I opened the door, Dad was in his studio and Ruffin's bark brought him upstairs. I stopped in my tracks when I saw his face.

"Dad! What happened?"

"It's Ozzie."

"What? What happened to him? Has he been arrested? Was he—?"

"Not yet, but he's acting like a fugitive. He's in hiding and won't tell me where. I think he's grieving more than actually hiding and he wants to be left alone. He called to tell me that he had Starr cremated."

"What?"

"That's right. So there'll be no funeral, no memorial service, no nuthin'. He has her ashes with him wherever the hell he's at right now. I mean there's nothing wrong with cremation if that's what he wanted to do but he seems to have really gone off the deep end; he's acting like a lunatic. I . . . I don't know what I can do. He needs help, and I—oh, man!"

I reached out and grabbed Dad's arm. "Listen. Sit down. Sit down." I led him to the sofa and we sat down together. Ruffin returned to his favorite spot in front of the fireplace, stretched out on the cool tiles, and stared at us, sensing that something was wrong.

"If I could only catch up with him. If I only knew—"

I listened, wishing that I had been home when the call had come in. Maybe I could've gotten a word, a hint of where he was.

"Can you imagine," my father continued, "Ozzie sitting alone at the crematorium, and God knows what thoughts were going through his head at the time? His only daughter dying the way she did and nobody but him to mourn her, not in privacy but in complete isolation. That's enough to send the sanest person over the wall."

I understood what Dad was saying, understood that if someone—anyone—didn't get to Ozzie soon, he would be lost, consumed by his own private rage. This was also affecting Dad, biting into the lines on his face, eating at him despite his best efforts.

"I'm going back out," I said. "See if I can find Too Hot. He usually hangs down at the Lenox Lounge when he's not at the club. Perhaps he knows something or someone who does."

Upstairs in my room I kicked off my high heels, abandoning my investigator persona, and slipped into a comfortable pair of mid-heels, suitable for long walks. I tend to walk everywhere because I never know what news I'll pick up along the way. I don't own a car because driving, I'd probably miss everything but the traffic lights.

The Lenox Lounge is an old, old bar on Malcolm X Boulevard between 124th and 125th streets which has somehow managed to hold on to its original Art Deco look since its doors swung open in 1939.

I stepped into the dark interior and made my way toward one of the red leather banquettes that curved in half-moon configurations against the wall opposite the long bar. Each booth was sectioned off by a soft-lit vertical column.

An archway of etched glass separated the back room, which held a grand piano and clusters of chairs and tables. This room, once called the Zebra Room because the walls had been covered with zebra skin, now exhibited glossies of Sammy Davis, Jr., Eartha Kitt, Lena Horne, Billie Holiday, and Sarah Vaughan, and silhouettes of Nubian princesses highlighted by small red wall lamps. The floor of small hexagonal white, gray, and terra-cotta tiles was still intact despite sixty years of heavy traffic. A leather ceiling, tanned from decades of cigarette smoke, accentuated the thirties ambience.

Too Hot was seated in a banquette near the jukebox and he signaled me to join him. He was seventy-two years old now and newly retired from his numbers enterprise but he still kept his eye on the action, still hung out in the jazz spots, clubs, and any restaurant that knew how to serve a good dinner. Now he sat sipping his usual Walker Black, straight up, and called to the barmaid, "I'll have another and bring this young lady an Absolut and orange, please."

As usual, he was dressed impeccably in a pale linen suit, dark cotton shirt, custom shoes, and his favorite five-hundred-dollar Panama rested on the table near his glass. He turned to me and I caught his smile in the dim light.

"So you was on that cruise. Musta been a real treat listenin' to all that jazz. I shoulda been there. By the time I'd made up my mind, the ship was sold out stem to stern. Couldn't even hitch a seat in the rowboat section. Your pop was tellin' me he played with the best. Good for him."

He shook his head in despair. "Next year, though, look out. I'm gonna take care a' business early, no more CPT for me."

I laughed. Mom used to say making plans on Colored Peoples' Time has caused black folks to miss out on every thing except bad luck. And the longer I lived, the truer it seemed.

"So how's Ozzie?" he said, changing the subject. "Is he hangin' in there? Damn shame about Starr. She was a beautiful girl. Smart, ambitious, got sidetracked for a minute but he had gotten her straightened out. That was a hell of a blow to have her die the way she did." He bowed his head, in sympathy, it seemed, and sipped his drink. He always sipped, and very slowly.

"Ozzie's taking it pretty hard," I said, lowering my voice even though the place had gotten crowded and no one was paying particular attention to us. The booths were filled and every seat at the bar was occupied.

Someone punched up the jukebox and Jeffrey Osborne's smooth sound drifted over the hum of conversation. "Can you woo-woo-woo?" he wanted to know.

I remembered the night Tad had virtually wiped out that CD. We had popped a bottle of bubbly for no particular reason other than we were together on his terrace and the breeze wafting off the river was soft and cool. The jasmine-scented candles had deepened the color in Tad's eyes and when he smiled, I felt the world slow down.

We listened to *You should be mine*... Over and over and over.

Until someone from a nearby terrace advised, "Brother, if the babe ain't ready by now, change your tune. Hit it or quit it so I can cop me a nod!"

We lowered the volume to a whisper, then all I heard was Tad's own whisper. I felt his breath in my ear and his hands moving in a warm slow dance over my stomach. "Can you woo woo woo?"

Ah, yes, indeed, sweetie. Yes, indeed. I could. There under the stars and in that soft breeze. Yes, indeed, I could.

"... so like I was saying, Mali, I don't know if Ozzie—"

"I'm sorry. What did you say?"

In the dim light, Too Hot squinted at me over the rim of his raised glass. "You feelin' all right? You lookin' a little dazed."

"A little tired, that's all," I lied.

"Maybe you need to chill out. Get on home and catch a wink."

"Not right now. I'm worried about Ozzie. He's disappeared and no one, not even Dad, knows where he is."

Too Hot put his glass down and leaned toward me. "Mali. Don't tell me he went and got to Short Change."

"I don't know. I thought you might've heard something."

Too Hot stirred his drink and looked around. The bar, already crowded, seemed to expand to accommodate several more people who had just entered and were now standing three deep at the bar. Some waved in his direction. He scanned them and waved back, then turned to me, shaking his head.

"Too early. But stick around. You know how things work."

I said nothing and made up my mind to wait.

"Now," he said, "what exactly are you lookin' for? No point in trackin' somebody, then when you find him, all you want to say is hello."

"Well, right now, that's all I have in mind. Ozzie's grieving more than he's hiding. And Dad's affected by all this. My father's about to fall apart."

I watched his face, trying to read it in the dim light. He took another slow sip before he spoke. "My favorite bass man and the best piano I ever heard might be out of action. Ain't that somethin'. Ain't that somethin'."

"So it's not just Ozzie I'm interested in," I said. "It's whoever might've been seen with Starr before she died."

"Well, like I said, stick around. You never know."

He was right. One never knows from one minute to the next what to expect. The barmaid returned to the table but I was still on my first drink. She waved and melted into the crowd again.

Someone changed up the menu and for the next half hour the jukebox pumped out the rhythm of the Afro-Cuban All Stars, vibrant stuff that made your foot itch to leap up and dance on the table. It was loud and strong and the volume of conversation rose accordingly, so loud that neither of us heard when the man approached our table.

"Hey, Hot, how's it goin'?"

Too Hot looked up and nodded. "Not bad. Not bad at all. Grab a seat and rest your feet. Want you to meet a friend of mine."

I looked from one to the other. Too Hot would not have invited him to join us to waste time.

"Mali, meet Sno."

I shook his hand and moved over to allow him to join us. I watched Too Hot signal the barmaid and like magic she materialized through the dense crowd.

"Set my man up. Whatever he's havin'."

"Harveys on the rocks, please," Sno said.

I stole a glance at him as he watched the rhythm of the girl's hips as she moved away from the table. Someone once said that if you knew ten people in New York, you knew everyone, and that seemed to apply particularly to the folks in Harlem. I knew that Sno's real name was Errol Coddington and that he was about 50 years old, had migrated from Antigua years ago and, after failing at several small retail ventures, had bought a pushcart and went into business as an ICEY vendor. I also knew that he worked two shifts: The daylight hours found him selling syrup-flavored snow cones to the kids and making a lot of money.

Early evening, when he had gotten his second wind and a fresh uniform, he hit the streets again around eleven. To make even more money. The fruit-flavored menu was changed up, night rates kicked in, and the snowcones came saturated with Bacardi Limon, Absolut Currant, Hennessy Cognac, Appleton Estate Special, Myer's Dark, and Dewar's White Label.

Sales were brisk but limited to the adults who lounged on

stoops and leaned out windows shooting the breeze and catching the news and who, like that famous dog, rushed to line the curb at the sound of the tinkling bell.

Sno made enough money to be highly selective. When a too-young or too-suspicious face approached, he switched to the emergency backup fruit flavors. He had a reputation to protect and it wouldn't do to have some angry parent chasing him down with a baseball bat.

Folks who love to boast about other folks' money said that Sno had a large investment portfolio. I only knew that he had real estate in Antigua, to which he retired every winter.

When the weather warmed, he returned to his three-story brownstone on 120th Street near Garvey Park to dust off his wagon and roll through the blocks again.

I knew all this and although he shook my hand politely, Harlem being what it is, I'm sure he knew me as the ex-cop who had sued the NYPD after being fired three years ago. There are few secrets here and most folks tend to live and let live.

"Mali was on that jazz cruise," Too Hot said, opening on a neutral note. Sno looked at me, smiling in the dim light. His face was dark and almost moon-shaped. His eyes appeared to be at perpetual half-mast but probably missed very little. When he spoke, there was a hint of island accent. "No kidding. How was it?"

"Pretty nice. My dad's group was in the lineup. Jeffrey Anderson." I said this with a trace of pride, knowing that he'd already made the connection.

"Oh. Oh, yeah. I know him . . . good bass man," he said. "Good sound."

"Ozzie Hendrix is his piano man," Too Hot said in the same low voice. "Shame what happened to his daughter."

I tried to watch Sno closely as Too Hot spoke and I thought I saw a flicker in his lidded eyes but he remained silent as Too Hot went on.

"That pimp got knocked the other day also. Rudy said crime goin' down but I wonder . . ."

"Probably messin' with those statistics like that captain did in the Bronx," Sno said. "You know they ain't reportin' all the stuff that go down unless it's somethin' spectacular. Somethin' that somebody gonna talk about."

"Not many folks talkin' about this," Too Hot said as he lifted his glass.

"Which one?" Sno asked.

"Starr Hendrix, Ozzie's kid."

"Cops think she may have been killed sometime between late Saturday night and early Sunday morning," I interjected. "Ozzie found her Monday afternoon when we returned. He hasn't been the same since."

"Late Saturday and early Sunday, you said?"

"Yes."

The waitress finally returned to place a small bottle of Harveys Bristol Cream sherry and a small, ice-filled glass on the table. Sno broke the seal, poured a drink, and took a sip. He did not say a word. The Afro-Cuban All Stars dropped their sound to a tune low and slow and the voices at other booths could be heard now. We three sat in silence and Sno's attention seemed focused on the people at the bar. I tried to think of something more to say but nothing occurred to me so I remained quiet and waited.

Finally he glanced at his watch and said, not to me, but to Too Hot, "Be talkin' to you soon."

Then to me: "Nice to meet you, Mali. Tell your Dad I like his sounds. I like 'em a lot. Tell 'im I like Ozzie too." And with that, he left the booth, made his way through the crowd, and was out the door.

Something had transpired but it was something I had missed because it was something unsaid, so I lifted my glass and concentrated on matching my small sips with Too Hot's. A minute later, I noticed the edge of a frown creeping over his brow. He tapped his fine, manicured fingers against the table and said, "Tell your pop to hang in there." Then just as quickly the frown disappeared: "So tell me more about the cruise."

He ordered another round and we listened to Nina Simone glide through a rendition of "Just in Time." Her voice seemed to pour from the jukebox like smoke.

I talked about Lou Rawls in the spotlight, his voice rolling over the crowd in waves, and how the applause rolled back, endless.

Too Hot closed his eyes, probably imagining the picture. Then Nina's voice again broke through the hum of conversation at the bar. "Don't take my teeth," she warned.

"Great. Great voice," Too Hot sighed, opening his eyes. "Too bad she singin' over there and not here. Haven't been here in years."

"Too bad," I agreed.

"Too bad about Starr, too. Nobody'll hear her ever again."

I thought about that and listened to Nina and thought about the aching hole someone had punched in Ozzie's chest.

The next day, Thursday, dawned with an overcast sky but it had cleared by the time I had showered, fixed Dad's breakfast, and taken Ruffin for a brief run in St. Nicholas Park. Dad had not been encouraged by my meeting with Too Hot and only grumbled when I told him about Sno.

"So he's got the word out. So what. You need to be putting some pressure on Tad. What's he doing about all this? Suppose Ozzie decides that suicide is the way out. He could've been saved if somebody had acted sooner."

"Dad, please. Ozzie's strong. He's not about to go that way. Trust me."

"Right now, I don't trust anybody or anything," he said and stomped down to the sanctuary of his studio, leaving me to sit in silence. I held my head in my hands. Suppose Dad was right? No one was there to prevent Ozzie from taking that way out. No one available to talk down the pressure of that soul-destroying anger. I closed my eyes tightly and a prayer came. *Hold on, Ozzie. Please hold on. You know we love you.*

Upstairs, I changed into a wrap skirt and sleeveless tee, then scanned my notebook. If I started out early enough, I could cover more territory than I had planned.

It had been after nine last night when I left the Lenox Lounge, too late to visit the Tuesday woman, Jeanette Beavers. Now I thought about how to approach her and the others. I was certain that Amanda had not called to alert any of them. She understood that my visit involved money—or the possibility of receiving some—so the pay-yourself-first-girl was smart enough to keep certain other things to herself. I put my notebook in my bag, grabbed my straw hat, and left the house.

The sun broke through the gray-edged clouds and Adam Clayton Powell Boulevard was bathed in radiant early morning light. Few people were out and the avenue was quiet enough for me to think about my next move. I needed to stick to my purpose: to get a clearer picture of Starr. For all the years I'd known her, apparently I hadn't known her well enough.

If I could understand her relationship with Short Change, then I could probably figure out some other stuff. I reminded myself that I needed to remain nonjudgmental. No preaching or teaching because these women could probably show me a thing or two.

I thought of different angles as I hurried along: Maybe Short Change decided to get Starr for her testimony. Maybe one of his other women had been jealous, had resented the fact that she broke out of the life and told their main man to kiss her butt. That kind of defiance probably had made the whole crew look bad. Or perhaps Travis was jealous of her, afraid of losing her. Maybe she had planned to free herself from him also. But why would he kill her that way when he could have used his gun?

Charleston had given me only vague descriptions of the women and I had no idea what to expect. I surmised or hoped that all of them would be taking a breather and trying to reassess their options now that their pimp was no longer in the picture.

I zigzagged my usual way through the side streets until I came to 123rd Street and Malcolm X Boulevard. At the corner, a sign under a large white cross erected in front of the Bethelite Community Church read: O.K. YOU WON THE RIGHT TO BE A LOSER. REJECT JESUS.

Jeanette Beavers lived in a four-story faded-brick walk-up across the avenue from the church. I climbed two flights and knocked on the door at the end of the dimly lit corridor. Footsteps moved softly behind the door and I heard an even softer voice: "Hello?"

"My name is Mali Anderson," I said, deciding to tell the truth. Or at least begin with the truth. Where I went from there depended on Jeanette.

"Mali who?"

"Anderson. I'm Starr's cousin and I need to speak to you about her father."

The door opened only as wide as the security chain allowed and I was able to glimpse an eye in a sliver of brown face.

"You from the police?"

"No. I'm trying to find out about my cousin Starr."

"What you want to know?"

"I'm not sure," I said, still trying to stick to the truth. The eye narrowed and inspected me and I felt like a character in one of those old-time TV gangster movies knocking on the door of an old speakeasy where the panel slid back, somebody eyed you, and the door opened to admit you into whatever particular fantasy that had compelled you to be there in the first place.

I waited patiently in the dim light, regretting now that I had not used the last will and testament tactic. The door would've sprung open by now. Then again, maybe not.

"Okay," I said, searching in my bag for my personal card. "If you think of anything, maybe you can give me a ring. Anything you remember will be—"

The door closed for an instant and I heard the chain slide back. "Come on in," she said, looking beyond me into the hallway. "Come on in."

I glanced behind me also, wondering if she was expecting anyone else. I stood inside her small foyer as she double-locked the door, then slammed a bolt in place.

"So where'd you get my name from?"

"From Starr's address book."

"Mmhmm. So you know the deal. She wasn't supposed to do that, keep different names and stuff. Ah, well, knowin' Starr, I ain't surprised. Nobody couldn't tell her nuthin'. She was her own woman from day one. Anyway, I'm in the kitchen. Come on. I'm havin' my third coffee and it ain't even noon yet. It ain't Starbucks, but it's good."

I followed behind her and saw that this apartment was also small but in sharp contrast to Monday's place. It was as if Jeanette had gone to Janovic Plaza Paints and gotten caught up in the store's announcement: "The sale of the day is pale dove gray."

It colored the walls and ceilings from one end of the apartment to the other. Additionally, the living room had a small pale gray sofa, an armchair upholstered in gray, the television was covered with a light gray scarf, the small square rug was pale gray, and the curtains were a gossamer gray.

I noticed that everything was extremely clean and precisely placed and there were no pictures to break the monochromatic cast of the walls. In the kitchen, the utensils and pots and pans were stacked in picture-perfect pyramids on shelves over the stove. And the fridge, which should've had at least one gray smudge, was as pristine as if it had been delivered yesterday.

Without asking, she reached into the cupboard and retrieved a gray cup trimmed in white and placed it on the table before me. "Have a seat," she said. "Now what's this about Starr's daddy? What's goin' on with him?"

Jeanette Beavers, otherwise known as Tuesday, was the kind of woman whose age would always be a mystery. She was about five feet six, with brown unlined skin, long fingers that were neither fat nor thin, and a face bare of makeup that looked almost pretty except for the dark circles under the eyes. Her light gray sweatsuit fit her and I didn't notice any lumps or bumps. With her high cheekbones and small nose, she could have been thirty years old or fifty.

"You know, I didn't mean to intrude on your privacy," I said, "but since Starr died, her father hasn't been the same. In fact, he's going downhill by the hour. Talking about doing something drastic."

She paused with the sugar dish in her hand. "Something drastic to who?"

"To himself," I said. "I can't let that happen. He and my dad are first cousins. Starr was my second cousin. Her father was upset when Starr got involved with Henry Stovall and—"

"—and he beat the shit outta Short Change," she said. "Ruined his rep. Yes, he did." She smiled at the remembrance, shaking her head. "I didn't see the outbreak but I saw the evidence. You shoulda seen Short Change. Couldn't hit the streets for weeks. And when he did, he cruised by real slow, real cool, lettin' everybody know that he was still on the circuit and nobody was gonna cut into his turf. And you know who he took it out on? Us. I mean, the man was like mad. We had to work twice as hard, bring home twice as much cash. And because he needed to show he was all right, he traded in his wheels even though it wasn't time yet.

"He usually do that every two years but he traded for the new one soon as it hit the showroom. Had it specially customized. He even got his own special salesman, you know."

Indeed I did. I listened and would have laughed if it wasn't so sad. His own special salesman. Just like those young new-money drug lords who strolled into those showrooms with pockets bulging and rolled out in models no other person in their right mind would even look at. Sixty-thousand-dollar vehicles "customized" with garish accessories and bizarre paint jobs to match their moronic mentality, and leaving behind a "special" salesman swimming in a river of money and straining to keep a straight face.

"How did Starr meet Short Change?" I asked.

Tuesday paused to turn the cup to her head and, hot as it was, didn't stop until it was half empty.

"Let's see. I'm not exactly sure but I heard she'd been sittin' in some bar or club waitin' for someone else. That someone never showed or was late showin' and she was gettin' mad as hell and Short Change sent a drink her way and then stepped over to calm her down. You know, he can talk fast, talk soft, and talk shit. That's his callin'. Make you think your life ain't been lived 'til he stepped into it."

"How long ago was that?"

"Two, maybe three years ago. She ain't last long, though. When she found out the real deal, she wasn't havin' it. Said she wasn't bein' no ho for nobody but her own self. Even tried to talk some of us out of doin' what we was doin'. I mean the girl was somethin' and wasn't scared of nuthin'.

"I think Short Change's pride was messed up, damaged by her. And it became a contest like, you know, who gonna come out on top of the game of life. He let her get away, especially after her daddy laid that pipe against his head. But he was schemin' the whole time. Let a month or so slide, then he eased back, determined to get even.

"As far as I could see, it wasn't even about Starr no more. It was about the two men. Him and her daddy, know what I'm sayin'? It was about payback time and Starr was the prize money. So he ran into her one night, probably been scopin' her out the whole time, then eased that slick talk on her and next thing you know, he had got her on that dope. Coke first, then heroin. It was bad, bad, bad. I mean, the girl went down to nuthin' 'til her daddy caught up with her and sent her away. Spent all them dollars to clean her up and look what happened."

"I know she went to court."

"Um-hmm. Testified against him. Told what she knew, which wasn't that much. Hell, none of us really knew that much about his other business. We had a certain amount of cash to bring in every night and that's all we mostly concentrated on, bringin' it in. What he did on the other side of town, we ain't had no time to find out."

"So her testimony didn't amount to much?"

"Not that I know of. Except to say that he had gotten her hooked, fed her her first shot."

I listened but didn't pull out my notebook. I would do that once the visit was over. "Tell me," I said, "how did Henry get the name Short Change?"

Tuesday had taken my now empty cup, scrubbed it until I thought the color would fade, then turned from the sink to look at me. "Don't you know?"

"Not really."

"Well, think about it, sweetie. That ain't too hard to figure out." She dried her hands and then glanced at her watch. "But looka here, I don't mean to rush you, but I gotta go. Somebody's waitin' and I don't like to be late."

I shrugged and gathered my bag. She smiled wide, eager to let me know that her current situation had changed radically and vastly improved.

"You know, when you first rang that bell, I thought you was one of the ho's from the stroll trying to recruit me. Some of the other pimps, they try to approach you, you know, sayin' your man checked out and left 'im holdin' this and that, you know, like a bill that ain't been paid. And if you dumb enough, they try to make you responsible, work for 'em 'til it's paid off. And everybody know that ain't never gonna happen. You be strollin' the rest of your life.

"Three of 'em already rolled up on me, tried that shit, and I told 'em to go fuck themselves. Let their bottom bitch take care of it. As far as I'm concerned, the script has flipped. I'm on my own. When I fuck, I keep the buck. That's my financial philosophy."

She put her own cup in the sink and went through the purifying process once more. "So like I say, sorry to rush you but I got a private-duty thing comin' up. And I got to get dressed to impress."

When I left the house, I crossed the avenue and waited near the sign in front of the church. A few minutes later, Tuesday stepped out of the house dressed simply in a light gray blouse, ankle-length black skirt, mid-high heels, and swinging a small patent leather bag on one arm and carrying an attaché case in the other. She looked nothing like the girls who strolled the Point near the Bronx Terminal Market. A taxi stopped, she climbed in, and I watched as the car headed downtown.

The car merged into the rush of traffic and disappeared before I left my spot. I glanced at my watch, surprised that it was almost noon. Malcolm X Boulevard was crowded now with fast-moving folks who seemed to care little about the heat. I had a choice: walk to 112th Street near St. Nicholas Avenue and try to visit Myrtle Thomas, the Thursday woman, or return home to see if Dad was all right. It was still early enough to do both and I decided to see about Dad.

A short distance from the corner of 133rd Street, I saw that the metal grill of Travis Morgan's computer store was pulled up. It was a wide storefront with windows on each side of a center entrance. The left window displayed an array of PCs, laptops, and small television sets. Travis's office occupied the space to the right of the door.

I decelerated to a crawl, slow enough to see that Travis was not there. Chrissie was. She was slouched in front of a computer, her face in profile, concentrating on the information scrolling before her.

I found myself changing course like a battleship in mid-ocean when it sights the enemy sub that had eluded it for so long. What I was prepared to say or do didn't matter because I was not prepared at all. But something inside me shifted, like tectonic plates, and allowed a vaporous substance, hot and dangerous, to bubble up. I ignored my voice of reason, usually too soft and too slow to matter, as it tried to dissuade me.

Mali, the cruise is over. Forget about what she did or what she said. It's over.

I listened instead to that other voice, the warring woman's. I always liked what she had to say.

Remember that lie she dropped on Miss Viv? Get her straightened out now, right now before it spreads any further. Who knows who else she's telling this stuff to? And besides, you're on home turf. Discretion is not a factor. Aboard ship you had to be cool. Didn't want to mess up Dad's rep by acting loud or drawing a crowd. Couldn't act colored, you know.

But you're home now, sweetie, and isn't it wonderful? It's showtime.

My shadow fell across her screen before the security chime sounded and when she looked up, I don't know who was more startled, she or I. She swiveled her chair but remained seated as I stared in surprise at her ashen face. Where had all those lines and creases come from?

It was as if she'd taken off a mask and finally revealed what lay beneath. Her neck looked like a chicken's and her shoulders sagged. She leaned away from the screen, and under that tight sleeveless sweater, the bra department wasn't holding up too well either.

Her eyelids were swollen and I wondered if it had been lack of sleep or too many tears. I stood there, at war with myself now, trying to decide if I should get right to it and slap her face, or apply a light cussing out, or, better yet, offer some soul-crushing observation that would send her running to the nearest plastic surgeon as fast as her credit cards could carry her.

Or just forget the whole idea.

She looked as if she'd stepped into the path of an SUV that hadn't a chance to brake.

We stared at each other and as it turned out, her surprise evaporated faster than mine.

"So what brings you to this neck of the woods?"

Even her voice had lost its sickly sweet pitch and now sounded as though she'd gargled with gravel.

"Nothing important," I said. "Just you."

"What about me?"

I saw this tête-à-tête moving into a twenty-questions session so I ignored her sad state and got to the point.

"Listen, Chrissie, I didn't appreciate the way you came on to my man aboard ship."

She leaned back and squared her shoulders in an attempt to resurrect at least a part of her old persona, but I looked at her sweater and slacks, an expensive set but in need of a serious size adjustment, not to mention style. The outfit, a floral-print number, was meant for a girl at least thirty years younger and thirty pounds lighter. Had we been on different terms, I would have taken her in hand and led her over to Eighth Avenue, where the

Afrocentric sisters of the Harlem Collective would have set her on the right track, then we would have breezed on over to Brooklyn, to Court Street, where the Gourd Chip sisters would have worked more fashion magic. As it stood now, Chrissie looked as if she'd fall apart if she sneezed.

I thought of Travis and what he'd said when he stepped out of Elizabeth's office: "The sooner the better."

I glanced at the spreadsheet but she pressed the screen saver, bringing on a tableau of floating bubbles. Though the print had been too small to read, I had the impression she was checking Travis's business accounts. Sometimes putting two and two together, I knew, could actually add up to the right number.

Despite Elizabeth's tight lips, I gathered that Travis had probably filed for a separation or a divorce. And here was Chrissie busily checking his assets. Sweet girl.

As tacky as she looked, I couldn't summon up an ounce of sympathy but I did the right thing and cut my conversation short with a warning: "I won't forget this," I said, and turned to leave.

But she was feeling bolder than she looked and her voice came at me like a missile from a slingshot. "Did you say 'your man'? *Your* man? I didn't notice any rings on him and don't see any on you now!"

I turned and was in her face in less than a blink. "Watch me tie a ring around your neck, you bitch!"

She scrambled out of her chair and edged around the desk. We faced each other, breathing fire, and before I could reach across the desk and rearrange her smirk, the bell chimed. We stepped to neutral corners just like pro fighters as a woman and two teenage boys walked in. One boy pointed excitedly at a laptop in the window. "See, Ma. That's the one. That's the one."

"Okay. Okay." The woman raised her hand for silence, looked

at me, then at Chrissie. "Can one of you help me? We're interested in—"

I did not reply and neither did Chrissie but the hard sound of her breathing filled the room. The woman's glance flitted between the two of us, probably trying to figure out what was happening. I ignored the woman and pointed a finger at Chrissie. "You and I will meet again," I said, and walked out the door.

The encounter slowed me down as I indulged in all the things I could've, would've, and should've said and done had I not been interrupted. Hindsight is good but all it did was make me angrier.

And I had to listen to the voice of reason again. That damn voice that said: Forget about it, Mali. Think about the cruise. The last few days were heaven. Chrissie drank too much and got sick, remember?

I remembered. I tried hard to concentrate but memory made me even angrier.

In Newport that Friday afternoon everyone was going ashore for the evening concert and I was glad, knowing that I wouldn't have to sit through another of Chrissie's dinner performances. The night before, she had ordered two bottles of champagne from the smiling sommelier and managed to polish off half of the first as if it were ginger ale. When I declined a toast, the Möet further loosened her tongue and she called me out on it.

"What's the matter? Afraid you'll lose something if you drink too much?"

Her filmy gaze had been glued on Tad, and everyone at the table waited, glasses poised. I waited also. Feeling Tad's hand under the table tighten on my thigh, his fingers sending me the signal to be cool, ignore her, I love you.

I concentrated on his hand as it slid along my knee, then I listened in the silence to my breathing, counting my intake of breath, relaxing. Breathing. Relaxing. Resisting the impulse to reach across the table and snatch that fall—or whatever they called those scraps of counterfeit hair that she had hanging over her shoulder—then snatch her sorry behind and throw her overboard.

But Tad's hand had moved to my thigh, where his fingers began to work magic at the top of my stocking. I sat there and smiled.

And before she'd managed to tip the second bottle she got sick. Right there at the table, she'd almost turned green and had to run to her room. My smile in the silence did not go unnoticed and the others declined a second round, probably convinced that I'd slipped a hex on the bottle.

Friday, everyone had assembled in the Grand Lounge and prepared to board the tenders for the concert on Goat Island. Tad noticed me scanning the crowd. "I know who you're looking for. Why don't you forget it?"

"I just want to make sure she's not on the same tender," I murmured. His eyes narrowed in irritation so I said no more. I did not mention that I'd gone to her cabin earlier to have it out with her once and for all. There was a Do Not Disturb Sign, which I ignored and knocked on the door. I heard music but nothing else, which was fine with me. I hoped she'd remain sick, I hoped she'd remain draped over the toilet all the way back to New York.

The evening breeze swept from the ocean and made me appreciate Tad's arm around me. Al Jarreau made me forget the earlier unpleasantness. Dad, who had been sitting with his own circle of friends, joined us on the trip back to the ship in time for the midnight buffet, which featured every chocolate dessert imaginable.

I took samples back to the cabin, fed Tad like a player in one of those old Roman orgies, and was amazed at what chocolate could do for your love life.

So you see, Mali, she got sick. You had a good time. Evil is as evil does.

The next day, again caught up in the crowds, the music, and the general excitement at Fort Adams, I could think of little else: Regina Carter, Branford Marsalis, and Chick Corea were standouts but it was Aretha, the queen, who blew us all away.

A hush fell over everything when her clear, perfect, soul-shaking voice sailed out and over the crowd, caught the current and swept the water, where hundreds of small craft, with decks crowded, had anchored.

I was wide-eyed behind my sunglasses, too afraid to blink, too afraid that this extraordinary moment would end too soon. And finally, when it did, I rested my head on Tad's shoulder and cried.

I opened the door and stepped into the sound of Miles Davis's "Doo-Bop", the set in which he had captured the sounds of the street, the urban sound, with the rapper Easy Mo Bee.

It was fast-driven wordwork undercut by Miles's leisurely instrumental riff. It filled the house and I stood there listening, imagining that everything was back to the way it should be. Hearing it meant that Dad felt well enough to concentrate. But he emerged from his studio looking the same—tired. Worn out.

"No word on Ozzie yet," he said, "but Tad left a message. Wants you to call."

In my room, I kicked off my shoes as I dialed his number, then just as quickly, before the dialing was completed, I hung up.

Not now. I'll only have to lie when he asks what I've been doing. And I don't want to do that. Not now.

I walked to the window and looked out, staring at nothing, listening to nothing, despite the chorus of sparrows and starlings in the trees that lined the curb.

You're not exactly dodging him, you know. Just do what you gotta do, what you planned to do, and then call him when you're done. It's not like outright lying...

It was Mama's voice. I closed my eyes. I no longer heard the birdsongs but I couldn't turn off the voice.

And I couldn't turn off the memory of Tad standing beside me on that wide deck in a black, quiet 3 A.M.

A moon hung low and bright against the night color of the water. We could not see the water, could only hear it, and imagine its depth.

"This is what it means to be out of this world," he had whispered. "Out of touch almost, with everything and everyone except the one most important person in my life."

His hand had circled my waist and I leaned into him, feeling the soft rhythm and roll of the deck as the ship sliced through the night. The quiet was unbroken and we had remained like that, so close that I could gauge the beat and rhythm of his heart. I thought of nothing and no one but him and a kind of peace, a complete and quiet state, settled over me.

I turned from the window and quickly slipped my shoes on, grabbed my shoulder bag, and was nearly out the door when Dad called from the kitchen, "Going out again?"

"Yes." I hesitated, then said, "Listen, if Tad calls again, tell him I'm still out, okay?"

This brought him from the kitchen, his face wrinkled with worry. "What's going on, Mali? Where are you off to?"

"Charleston gave me a few names," I said, not wanting to go into too much detail and certainly not ready to tell him what these folks did for a living. "I'm going to contact one more person, then head back home."

"Mind telling me where this person lives?"

"No problem."

I wrote the name and address on a slip of paper and slipped out the door as he studied it. "Back in an hour. I promise."

I headed downtown, a fast walk without too much to see except a young man at the corner of 128th Street busily beating a public phone to death in lieu of the twenty-five-cent refund. If he had been armed, he probably would have shot it.

The plaza of the Harlem State Office Building at 125th Street was crowded with people lounging in the afternoon sun.

On 116th Street, the dome of the mosque that Malcolm X once headed cast a shadow on the row of stores and restaurants that defined Little Africa.

I cut through 114th Street, where I passed Alvin's school. Wadleigh High, now coed, was the first public high school for girls chartered in New York, and actresses Jean Stapleton and Anna Marie Horsford are alumna of this national landmark.

The closer I came to 110th Street, Harlem's gateway, the more impressive the housing appeared. What would have been described as tenements a few years ago now had restored entrances flanked by huge planters overflowing with flowers and protected by gleaming iron railing. Young trees and clipped shrubs lined the immaculate sidewalks and I wondered where the old tenants had gone and what the new rents were like.

At 112th Street, St. Nicholas Avenue converged with Malcolm X Boulevard. At the apex, I found Myrtle Thomas's house, a tall gray building facing a small supermarket across the street. There were several upscale businesses in the area, including an accounting firm, a bakery, and a popular catering hall facing the northern perimeter of Central Park.

The entrance to Myrtle's house was also decorated with planters. I couldn't tell the age of the flowers but the stone containers looked new. The front door was fashioned of etched glass set in oak and I paused to scan the narrow bronze strip listing the tenants. Her name was not there but there was one blank slot. I took a chance and pressed the bell next to it.

I thought about what I was going to say into the intercom and decided to be up front if indeed it was her bell. That was the fastest and easiest way. If she didn't agree, then the hell with it. Move on.

I was surprised when the buzzer sounded. I stepped quickly into the foyer and the carpet felt thick under my feet. The light from the wall sconces was soft enough to take at least ten years off my face when I glanced into the pier mirror at the end of the corridor. I didn't look too long before a door a few feet from the mirror opened and a woman stepped out.

"Oh," she said. "Did you ring? I thought—"

"I'm sorry," I said. "I did ring. I'm looking for Myrtle Thomas."

Her expression, not exactly soft to begin with despite the benign lighting, took on the substance of rock. This was the Thursday woman. She was as tall as I, about five feet nine, but built with the kind of sturdiness that forecasted an eventual battle of the bulge. Her brown face was framed by a halo of auburn hair and at one time, I supposed that she had probably been very pretty. When she opened her mouth, her voice was as hard as her face. "Who are you?"

"My name is Mali Anderson and I'm Starr Hendrix's cousin. I need to ask—"

"How did you get my name?"

"From her notebook."

"Starr's dead. What do you want?" Thursday had placed her hands on her hips, a sign that told me to go slow or go back home.

"I know Starr's dead," I whispered, hoping to bring her voice down to a more normal range. "I'm here because of her father."

"I don't know him. What do you want from me?"

"I . . . I just need . . . to talk to you, or to someone, anyone," I whispered, putting on my best bereaved expression. "Her father, he's an old man, still in shock. I don't know if he'll ever get over this. I need to find a way to help him, I need to be able to tell him something."

She looked at me and although her expression was still as sour as last month's milk, she opened the door wider and jerked her thumb, beckoning me inside. I entered, wondering if this was a good idea, but, well, what the hell . . .

The apartment was completely bare, the only available sitting space a small crate among the boxes and cases that crowded what was once the living room. There was no furniture and no lamps and the ceiling fixture highlighted gray outlines of several pictures that had been removed from the walls.

"You caught me just in time. I got one more thing to do tonight and tomorrow I'm out of here."

I didn't ask her destination, not yet anyway, but stood near the door leading into the kitchen. That also was empty of furniture and probably of food.

"I thought you were the delivery guy," she said. "I ordered take-out a half hour ago."

I nodded and waited as she rummaged through her bag and took out a cigarette.

"Okay, so you're Starr's cousin. What's wrong with her old man?"

"Well," I said, undecided where to go with this, "he never understood her, didn't know what drove her to do the things she did."

"You're kiddin'. Hell, if he didn't know, and he's her old man, how you expect somebody else, a stranger, to know?"

"You're right," I murmured. "It's just that when there's no answer, it's hard to—"

"Ahh, what the hell," she whispered, more to herself than to me. Once she got started, she talked fast, picking at memory, and seemed in a rush to get it all out and over with. As if talking about it now would acquit her of ever having to mention it again.

"I ain't gonna be here anyway so . . . Well, I don't know that much but let me tell you this. I first met Starr when Henry was tryin' to turn her, but she was so tough, so strong, even with the Vegas treatment."

"The Vegas treatment?"

"Yeah. The three of us went for a weekend. Always somethin' big happenin', which meant ready steady money. Starr was still the princess so he strolled the strip, talkin' his talk, showin' her all the lights and shit, and gettin' her to dream in Technicolor about how it was gonna be.

"I was supposed to play backup like usual, you know, tellin' her all what she was gonna get if she played her game correctly. Instead, she wound up tellin' me what I was supposed to be doin'.

"So Henry sent me on private duty—two hundred dollars an

hour—and said he was gonna convince her by himself. I told him he was wastin' his time.

"After I had made my first four or five thousand, I told him we should head back east and leave her ass right there to leg it home the best she could. Let her fuck her way back. But she woulda probably called her daddy and he woulda flew out to rescue her like some white knight. Or is it a white horse, I forget which."

Myrtle's laugh was short. "Well, I don't know what happened. Most pimps woulda walked away, wrote her off if she couldn't bring in that fast money, but Henry saw her as some kind of challenge, though to this day, I can't figure out why."

The cigarette hung in her mouth unlit as she searched her bag for her lighter. She gave up and leaned over the stove at an angle, turned on the jet, and lit the cigarette that way. Then she stood erect and drew in a deep breath of smoke.

" 'I can't lose with the stuff I use,' he liked to say. Only thing was his stuff wasn't workin'. Not that time. I mean he was a fast talker and he nearly had her. It shoulda been easy."

She took a long drag and I looked at her and wondered how anything could have been easy. From what I'd heard, Starr had been one single-minded sister. Myrtle drew in another lungful and I watched the smoke trail from her nostrils as if she were one of those old-time silent-screen movie stars.

"Henry—Short Change—was the kind of man who could tip into your dreams," she continued. "I mean waking dreams, not like in the midnight hour—that time was for makin' sure a woman knew what and how to do what she was supposed to do. But past that time. More toward dawn. When life is pink with possibilities. He'd tap into those early A.M. dreams, plans, and hopes, and he'd whisper, 'I can make it happen, baby.' All the while, his hands is steady workin', movin' up and down, and his fingers mixin' in your money maker and pretty soon you think it's all gonna be as good as that . . ."

All you got to do is . . .

As Myrtle spoke, I imagined a trap sliding open wide and silent and a clawed hand reaching out.

". . . at least," she continued, "that's the way he usually worked it. He could talk the talk but he soon found out that so could she. And it wasn't too long before she told him to kiss her ass."

"Starr said that?"

"Yes, indeed, she did. Your cousin's the only one I know that said somethin' like that to his face and didn't get beat. But I guess he got back in other ways."

"The drugs?"

"Yeah. That's what he did. Then when she went to court, that really blew it."

"You think he did her in?"

Myrtle looked at me, took another lungful of smoke, and shrugged.

"Who knows? She had her other man, didn't she? Coulda been him. Or it coulda been some other pimp or dealer or somebody who had it in for him and everybody connected with him. Coulda been anybody, way I see it."

The bell rang, startling us both. This time she went to the intercom and pressed the button to speak.

I heard a garbled response and she pressed the buzzer to allow the caller to enter.

"I'm leavin' for Vegas tomorrow night," she said, stubbing the cigarette in the kitchen sink. "Some a' that big money got my name on it and I mean to claim it."

I didn't respond but wondered what she was going to do and how long she'd be able to do it. Vegas had young girls by the busloads coming in every hour, some as young as fourteen or fifteen, and the woman standing before me, hard times not withstanding, appeared to be close to forty. On a good night with the right light she could perhaps shave off five years. Perhaps. My hope was that she'd learned a little something from Starr and stashed some of that fast cash. She was going to need it.

Myrtle returned my stare. "You know, since you her cousin, how come there ain't been no wake for the girl? How come we ain't hear nothin' about no funeral or something?"

Before I could answer, she said, "You know what we did? We gonna meet tonight, before everybody split up. Gonna have our own thing. Martha was already gone, went home and married a preacher. Ain't that too much? But I called and she flew back up just for this. We gonna do this just the way I think Starr would've done it for one of us. I don't know where Sara Lee is, but most of us will be there."

"May I come?" I asked, not knowing where this meeting, this wake, would be, and hoping it wouldn't be someplace where I might have to step out of a fourth-floor window if the situation got tight.

Myrtle lit another cigarette and sized me up and I quickly added, "Her dad, he isn't in his right mind right now. Starr didn't have a funeral. He had her cremated and went there and sat all alone until it was over. He loved Starr but that was the only wake she had and I didn't even know about it until it was all over."

"He did that? Sat in that place all by himself?"

I shook my head. "No funeral and no wake."

"Damn! That's some deep stuff."

"He isn't in his right mind," I said again and added, "If I can just tell him something, you know, that might bring him back, something good that he'd like to hear about her."

The bell rang and when she opened the door, the aroma told

me that she had received take-out from Charleston and that Jo Jo was standing at the threshold. As Myrtle went to get her purse, I stepped into view and pressed my finger to my lips. We looked at each other and nodded like two strangers who might have once occupied space on the same elevator.

Maybe Charleston's ribs and secret sauce had something to do with it but there was a fissure in Myrtle's gravelly attitude after she ate. She agreed to let me accompany her and we left the apartment.

On Lenox Avenue, it had grown dark and the night folks were coming out, looking for the usual excitement that comes with the dark. Blinking lights flashed from small bars and posters promoted the local jazz groups. The street was crowded and excitement blew through the air like barely contained steam.

I was pulled by twin currents of music and

laughter and understood what Dad meant when he described a time when "folks with nowhere to go got all dressed up and went to heaven just walking along Lenox on a summer night."

"So we meetin' in this little hangout," Myrtle said, cutting into my thoughts. "It's kinda a out-of-the-way place where not too much is goin' on. We like it 'cause it's quiet and sometimes that's what we need. Quiet."

At 117th Street, a few doors from the busy traffic of the avenue, we stepped into a small, dimly lit storefront that had no sign on the outside, just a small yellow light in the window, its weak glow slicing through the blinds as an invitation for those who knew what was happening.

Inside was crowded with a half dozen small tables covered with checkered cloths. In the rear, a wooden counter served as the bar. The lighting was so dim, anyone on the lam could lounge in comfort and not be positively ID'd for at least six months.

There was a large fridge and an icemaker and though there were no bottles in evidence, I knew the liquor was stocked under the counter. On the wall behind the bar, a large fluorescent-lit sign read:

NASHEELA NORRIS BRAITHEWAITE

BETTER KNOWN AS LITTLE DUMPLIN'

IS WANTED

DEAD OR ALIVE

BY THE DEPARTMENT OF HEALTH

AND FORMER BOYFRIENDS

IN CONNECTION WITH A INFECTION

Spots like these, I knew, were usually operated by biker clubs, or the neighborhood numbers guys, or simply functioned as a place to hang and knock back a brew without the bother or benefit of a liquor license. As long as there were no murders and the mayhem was minimal and the cops got their cut, the place was allowed to remain open. The spot, I found out later, was called just that—the Spot.

Three tables along the right wall had been pushed together to accommodate Monday (Amanda Johnson); Tuesday (Jeanette Beavers); and Friday (Martha Golden, who had returned for the occasion), and they all looked up as Myrtle and I approached.

Monday, especially, cut me a look that had the B-word tattooed all over it.

"Where's the ladies' room?" I said, looking directly at her. The pay-yourself-first girl got the message and rose from the chair even before the intros were finished.

"I'll show you!"

I nodded and followed her down a narrow passage in back of the counter, impressed that the voice of a girl her size could have so much volume.

The ladies' room, such as it was, was only large enough to hold one commode, a miniature wash basin with no soap in sight, a small cracked mirror over the basin, and one thin roll of toilet tissue held to the wall on a wire coat hanger. The bathroom was designed for one, but we both squeezed in.

I had intended to explain my presence and ask her to be cool but when she spoke, I knew she had already been drinking, and so standing face-to-face in the closet-size space was not the most pleasant experience, especially when her hand slid up from her side holding a switchblade.

"So what you doin' here, bitch? Why you lyin' sayin' you Starr's cousin? What the fuck is goin' on?"

She had pressed the blade against my stomach, prepared to push it in. I had two options: Take the knife away and slice her with it to teach her a lesson, or take the knife, drop it outside, then whip her scrawny behind for being so stupid. She was half my height and weight and the space was so small, she had very little room to maneuver, knife or no knife.

I chose option three and grabbed her hand just above the wrist and bent it back so fast, the knife fell to the floor as my other hand went to her throat and slammed her head into the wall.

"Now you listen to me. I'm her cousin, dammit. And I really do work for the attorney who's investigating that insurance claim, you understand? And I don't like surprises, especially sharp ones in small spaces."

I underestimated my grip on her throat and she appeared ready to gag. I wasn't about to have any secondhand alcohol ruining my dress so I relaxed my fingers and she coughed long and loud. When she was able to speak, she said, "You tell any of 'em about that policy?"

"No. Their names are not on it. Why would I mention it? And I don't expect you to mention it either, you understand? I'm Starr's cousin and to hell with the policy and the money and everything connected with it. I'll just tell the attorney that I've been threatened and to close the investigation."

Her eyes grew wide. "What happens to the money? Who gets it then?"

"It goes to the State of New York," I said, "one hundred and fifty thousand dollars."

"What?"

"That's right. It'll go where a lot of unclaimed money goes when folks act stupid."

In the dim light, I could see the tears gather, but I didn't know if it was because of Starr or the impending loss of the money or the fact that she had nearly been choked senseless.

Greed won out and she whispered, "Damn. I didn't know

what I was doin'. Look, I'm . . . sorry. I don't want this to go any further outside this room."

"I'm sure you don't," I said, opening the door and stepping out to breathe relatively fresh air. She remained inside, probably searching in the dim-lit space for the knife. I returned to the table and took a seat at the other end, as far away from her as I could get.

A CD player on the counter was playing "Darling Nicky," an old lament by The Artist Formerly Known As Prince, and everyone at the table was trying to talk above it. Finally Myrtle called out, "Can we turn that damn screamin' down? It ain't like we at some fuckin' Meadowlands concert!"

"That mouth gotta be Myrtle," the bartender yelled as he adjusted the sound. "I'd know that 'fuck' anywhere."

"Well then, fuck you!" she cried. "And gimme a drink while you at it!"

I looked from one to the other. A knife had been drawn in the bathroom. Now here was more loud and loose talk that might or might not end in a throw-down. And the quiet evening hadn't even begun.

The switchblade artist returned to the table and slipped into her seat and avoided looking in my direction. The bartender, a clean-headed short dark man in his late sixties with a round stomach, approached the table and plopped down two plastic buckets of ice, then wiped his hands on his shirt.

"Okay, talk to me, ladies."

"I'm havin' Dewar's tonight so I don't have no hangover tomorrow," Myrtle said.

"And I'm havin' me a vodka and orange soda," Jeanette smiled, " 'cause I know you ain't got no juice."

The bartender looked at her and a smile flickered.

"I got plenty juice, baby . . ."

"Yeah? What flavor you got?"

"What flavor you want?"

"See. I told you he ain't got no juice. Gonna gimme some a' his private stuff."

"Baby, you know I'm still young, dumb, and full a' come."

Amid the laughter, Jeanette leaned back, squinted, and focused her sights on the spot below his potbelly, holding her hand over her brow like a sailor searching the horizon and finding nothing.

"Man, you so old, what you got I can't hold. Just gimme a orange soda. At least I can taste that and belch some gas afterwards."

"Awh, girl. One a' these days you gonna break my heart."

He moved, still laughing, to take the rest of the orders. I didn't bother to specify the brand of vodka I wanted because I knew that Absolut, Smirnoff, and Stoli would all be poured from the same five-dollar-a-gallon jug.

He returned with a tray loaded with enough alcohol to intoxicate an army. The liquor had been poured into eight-ounce plastic cups and three cups were placed in front of each of us.

"Hey," he said, placing more ice and then the chasers on the table, "tonight is three for one and since y'all here to wake Starr, lemme know if you need some chips and stuff."

Everyone lifted a cup in a toast. I took a quick sip of something that bore no relation to vodka and quickly put the cup down. Everyone else drank and the talk began.

Amanda started off as if she had been earlier interrupted and now continued without pause:

"—and y'all know truth from a lie. Sure I wanted something but I had to get out of there to get it. Woman lyin', sayin' I tried to take her husband. Fuck her. He didn't want her and I didn't want him and so far as I was concerned, we all was even. I couldn't help it if I was half her age. I ain't had nuthin' to do with God's plan. I mean, the man put all a' them dollars in my lap 'cause my titties stood up better than his wife's ever did. He said so. So why she jump bad with me? She shoulda got down on her knees and prayed for a new set. And she shoulda sliced him, not tried to get at me.

"Anyway, he didn't have enough for me so I left. I knew what I needed and intended to get it. One way or the other. Do or die. Even Short Change with all his slick talk was for me just a short stop on a long road."

The voices rose in approval and Jeanette, the Tuesday woman, looked at her. "You was kinda young to be so grown but I guess that's what Short Change liked. That's what he liked about Starr too. Until sister got bad enough to tell him to kiss her royal black ass.

"You know what Short Change said to me one night?" She raised her cup, frowning in remembrance. "Said get all you can while you can 'cause tomorrow's dollars ain't promised. Work it 'til you hurt it and by that time it won't matter 'cause by then you'd have made your million and you can quit. You can quit. Ain't that some shit?"

"Did he say that?"

"Did he?"

The laughter drowned out the opening chords of "When Doves Cry," the best record that Prince ever made. I hadn't heard it in years and with all the noise, it was unlikely that I would hear it now.

Myrtle, the Thursday woman, broke into their laughter. Her voice had that cigarette rasp, as if she had just gone through an entire carton nonstop.

"I was special," she said. "When I met him, I knew I wasn't goin' out on no stroll. Not me. When I hooked up, I came with names and numbers, private, unlisted shit. Didn't have to fight that heat and snow and wonder if I was gettin' into the wrong car and end up bein' rolled out on the other side of a highway. Not me. I was in demand from the best men. Downtown men who couldn't tire you out even when they sweated like hogs. They were the strangest, the ones who sweated and begged you to do the strange shit."

She lit a cigarette and the smoke rose in a white spiral. "It beat workin' as a live-in and havin' to fuck the man of the house for free while his wife went off to her bridge game. I mean I got paid, but not for what I did, but for what I didn't say when the woman come trottin' back home. Shit, the grin on her face make me think she was out probably fuckin' somebody's husband her own self. When I saw how much I could make just by leanin' back? Girl, please. Instead of turnin' mattresses, I was layin' on 'em. Nice, soft, expensive ones."

"Yeah, but Starr wasn't havin' none a' that," said Martha.

"Well, she didn't need to," Jeanette said. "She come from a different thing altogether." She turned to me now. "You her cousin. Tell us how come she hooked up with Short Change."

"Starr wanted to be just that. A star," I said. "She had a damn good voice and wanted to sing. I don't know what Short Change said to her but once she got hooked on the drugs, everything else went out the window."

"That's 'cause she wasn't havin' none a' Short Change's program," Martha Golden, the Friday woman, said.

Like Amanda, Martha also appeared to be barely out of her teens, with small features, smooth dark brown skin, and short processed hair that gave off an unnatural glow in the dim light. Her voice was soft and her manner seemed slow and thoughtful, but it was hard to ignore the jackhammer toughness lurking just below the surface.

"Short Change was just one more son of a bitch, far as I'm concerned," she said. "When I met him, bad things had been happenin' to me for so long I figured one more thing wouldn't make much difference. My mama was the kind who saw and didn't see, you know what I'm sayin'. Her man wasn't my father. He helped himself to both of us and she didn't do a thing. Nothing. Didn't want to disturb her happy home. Kept her eyes closed and her mouth shut and had his kids fast, like rabbits, and all along treated me like I was the outside one.

"Well, the last time when he come at me, I grabbed my blade and sliced him three ways: Long. Deep. And serious. Mama, she hear the commotion and come bustin' in, saw what the deal was, but she slapped me instead. The bitch slapped me! Well, I went off, you hear me. Read her dumb, blind ass while he rollin' on the floor, blood splashin' everywhere. And I really was outside from then on.

"I kept steppin' and made up my mind that when I went back, I was goin' in style. That's what I lived for. And didn't I do it, baby? Didn't I do it?"

"Yes, you did." Everyone raised their cups now. "You damn sure did."

"Damn right I did. Married that old preacher man who been after me all his life and built us a house so big you could drive a bus through it and not touch anything.

"No, I don't love him the way I should because I don't know how, but he treats me right and I'm gonna learn. Meanwhile, the stuff I lay on him make him go to sleep with a groan and wake up with a grin."

The sound of the CD had lost out and the bartender turned it down so low, only he could hear it. He sat at the bar sipping a beer and snapping his fingers in time to an imperceptible beat. He was the only other person in the place, though I imagined as the night wore on, especially toward dawn, the place would be packed.

The first cups were empty and everyone had started on the second round. The chorus grew louder:

"Girl, that was some deep shit!"

"Me, I wouldn'a taken it!"

"Oh, yes, you would have."

"No, there comes a point where you—"

"Well, she cut the mother fucker, didn't she?"

"Don't tell me—"

"Reminds me of somethin' Starr woulda done."

"Damn, I miss her."

"Just think, if we had listened to her, we'd probably be unionized and them fuckin' pimps would be on the unemployment line."

Amanda broke in again. "Listen, we here to wake Starr. Not to talk about no fuckin' pimps."

"Well, what's a ho without a pimp?"

"Fuck you!" Amanda jumped up and I thought the thugette was going to bring out her carver. "Starr was no ho," she cried. "That's what got her killed!"

"How you know what got her killed unless you did it?" Tuesday said.

Amanda stared at her openmouthed, then leaned forward, placing her hands on the table. "Listen, bitch, what're you tryin' to say?"

"I'm sayin' you was jealous of Starr and you know it! Ain't nobody was more jealous than you," Tuesday shot back. She had risen quickly and despite the amount of alcohol, she was steady on her feet and ready for a fight. "Starr quit 'cause she wasn't takin' no shit. You got beat every time S.C. looked at you."

I glanced at the bartender sitting on his stool with his back against the wall. His eyes were at half-mast and he remained silent, as if this spectacle was nothing new. He was probably waiting to see who would make the next move before he reached behind the counter for his bat.

"Both a' y'all shut the fuck up," Thursday shouted. "Starr ain't quit. You got to be in somethin' to quit somethin' and all of us except her was in up to our tired tonsils. We—"

"What you mean I got beat?" Amanda persisted, ignoring Thursday's opinion. Her thin nostrils flared like wings and I thought she was going to take off and crash against Tuesday like a kamikaze.

"You did. Tried to play him and got beat," Tuesday answered, enjoying the tantrum.

Amanda's hands flew to her hips and she drew herself up to her full five-feet-three-inch height. "Well, lemme tell all you ho's somethin'. I got some licks but I got some cash too. Got more cash stashed than all y'all put together."

"What a liar."

"Who you callin' a—?"

Suddenly a soda can crashed in the middle of the table. Thursday lifted it again and held it high, preparing to bring it down once more.

"All y'all mother fuckas listen up. If it was anybody did it, it was S.C."

A silence followed. I watched Jeanette move her cup over the table cloth, concentrating on the checkerboard pattern. "You on the money," she whispered. "I always thought Short Change did it, or had somethin' to do with it. I'm glad the motherfucker got taken out."

The tension at the table did not entirely evaporate but lowered to a simmer, ready to flare up at the snap of a misdirected finger.

But the women nodded, synchronized, it seemed, to the idea

that it could have been their pimp who'd knocked Starr off. Myrtle spoke up: "I ain't so sure about that. The only one who'd know the real deal is Sara Lee. She the one used to live with him."

"Well, who knows where Saturday is? Got kicked to the curb and probably dead by now."

This brought another moment of silence. I looked at each in the dim light and saw not reflection but fright, a moment in which each was probably looking at her own future.

Four men strolled in, took seats at the bar, and checked us out. Myrtle and Amanda recognized them and waved and two of them brought their cups to the table. Their presence ended the wake.

I rose to leave, knowing that Myrtle would eventually fill in the story of Starr's cremation. This had not been a wake but an alcohol-soaked, feel-good session full of self-congratulation for having survived life with, and the death of, S.C.

And Starr had been done in by him because she told him to kiss her ass. Not likely. I had to find Sara Lee, the Saturday woman.

15

A light rain had come and gone but folks who were usually out at 2 A.M. had retreated indoors and stayed. Cabs had also disappeared at the first drop and didn't return.

I walked uptown in the quiet, imagining the life of Myrtle and Jeanette, Amanda and Martha. Except for Amanda, how much money had any of them saved? Except for Martha, what were their plans? Myrtle was headed for Vegas but how long would she last?

Most of all, I wondered about Starr's life. I wasn't her cousin, but I knew her. Or thought I did.

Powell Boulevard was deserted and I walked fast, listening to my footfalls echo behind me.

Despite the glow of the streetlights, Strivers Row, with its abundant trees, seemed darker in the mist. I quickened my pace. Several doors from my house I heard something: a swift, sliding shuffle, and a second later my neck was snapped back in a choke hold.

No sound, just a deep intake of breath—maybe my own. I couldn't yell, couldn't scream, but I struggled, driving my elbow into a hard stomach. I flung my purse away. If the mugger wanted it, he would have to scramble, and maybe give me enough room to kick his ass. His hand, large as a bear's paw, clamped on my nose and mouth, cutting my breath.

We grappled and I dropped to one knee and brought him with me, throwing him off balance. I broke, spun around, and drove a hard right to his stomach as he staggered to his feet. He was my height but much heavier, and only his eyes and mouth showed through his ski mask.

I found my breath and screamed, knowing that Dad was too far away to hear but maybe someone else would. Still screaming, I aimed for the eyes but he feinted and came in low, nearly knocking me off my feet. I grabbed the mask and pulled it as we fell against the hedge but his features were a blur in the dim light.

Windows suddenly slammed open, blazing with light.

"Hey! What's going on out there?"

Doors opened. "What's happening?"

The man leaped away and started running. He made it to the avenue and rounded the corner as neighbors in their nightclothes poured out of their houses. Two men ran after him, one waving a baseball bat and another with his hand in his bathrobe pocket, and I knew without asking what he was carrying.

I was sitting on my stoop trying to catch my breath and make sense of what had happened when they returned to join the small crowd gathered around me.

"He got away, Mali. Did you get a look at him?"

"Think you'd recognize him if you saw him again?"

Another neighbor had retrieved my shoulder bag, handed it to me, then stepped away from the sound of Ruffin's barking.

"Your dad's at the club," a woman in the crowd said. "I saw him leave. You want me to call him?"

I raised my hand. "No. No. I'm all right. I'll tell him when he gets home. Should be any minute."

"Well, long as you all right."

"Tell you what," added the bat man. "You go on inside. I'll pull guard duty 'til Jeffrey gets here. You step inside and try to quiet Ruffin down."

I left him on the stoop practicing as if he were ready to step to the mound at Shea.

Inside I leaned against the door and closed my eyes. The man was someone I knew. Or someone who knew me. Before he ran, he had breathed in my ear, "Round one is yours, bitch!"

I coaxed Ruffin over to the fireplace, where he finally calmed down, but minutes later I saw his ears perk up, and he was on his feet heading to the door as the rotating flash of light spun through the curtained windows. Someone had called the cops and I was not happy about it.

If they were regulars from the precinct, the ones who knew my history, they would be happy to see me covered with bruises. I glanced in a mirror before I opened the door. No marks visible yet. I was still in good shape. I opened the door slowly and looked at the Mutt and Jeff team lounging against the banister.

"Trouble here?"

I looked at them and wondered if they had ever glanced at that "Courtesy, Respect, and Professionalism" logo painted on the side of their cruiser. Some public relations firm really hit the jackpot with that account. All pay and no work.

What few questions they asked, I answered quickly. I did not invite them in. They glanced at Ruffin and did not insist.

"The assailant was tall, one hundred ninety pounds, late twenties, with a dark ski mask," I said.

"He say anything?"

"The mask muffled it," I said, knowing how happy they'd be to learn that I'd been assaulted, threatened, and robbed. The short cop—so vertically challenged that I thought he was interviewing my chest—busied himself with the incident report.

Once I gave my name, he needed no other information. He knew of me and his pen flew across the page. Address, phone, occupation. He paused here, waiting until I said certified social worker. He knew about the lawsuit—few cops in the precinct didn't. And some of them were still steaming.

"He did not get my purse," I said, bringing the interview to a quick close. I locked the door and listened to their footsteps on the stoop. I heard their voices as they questioned the bat man, then advised him to get rid of the bat. I opened the door again, quickly, and remained there as he replied:

"Oh, man. I didn't think of that. Thanks for the advice. If the street crime unit show up, that would really be something, wouldn't it?"

The cops looked at us, then at each other, and left the stoop. The motor revved, and a minute later the flashing lights faded. The bat man winked and remained where he was.

"Can I fix you some coffee, Mr. Sam?"

"Naw, honey. I'm fine. You go on do what you got to do."

Back inside I eased onto the sofa and felt pain arc up my back and settle like a large rock on my shoulders. I was too wired to close my eyes and that parting remark spun in my head like a middle-of-the-night alarm that wouldn't shut off. "Round one is yours, bitch!"

Dad sat in the chair and squeezed his eyes shut. He held his head in his hands and groaned as if he had been hit as hard as I.

"Mali? What . . . ?"

He could not speak and I rushed to fill in the silence. "I'm all right, Dad. Nothing serious happened. It was some crackerjack chasing the pipe and desperate for money. That's how it happened. There was no weapon. Just the mask. Probably pulled so many muggings his face is known all over by now."

My father nodded but I looked in his eyes and saw that he didn't believe my explanation. No one ever used a mask, unless they were robbing a bank. Dad was frightened, tired, so much so that I could not bring myself to repeat the message, the parting shot the man left to float in the coil of my imagination.

I still felt the assailant's breath on my face and I needed to take a bath. I managed to get Dad settled, then I filled the tub with a mix of hyacinth bubble bath and aloe, put on a CD of Aretha, and lay back to digest all that had happened. The water was warm and Aretha's voice was so soothing, it was easy to close my eyes just for a second. But no sooner had I nodded off than I was back on deck.

It was midnight and I was alone. A storm had blown in, washing the deck, and the sea foamed in glistening black bubbles around my ankles. I staggered, lurched as if one leg were shorter than the other. Branford Marsalis's clear notes blew above the waves and I wanted to yell for help but sound was locked in the back of my throat.

Near the pool, someone grabbed at my arm. It was Starr, small and brown and so pretty that even the wet, ragged evening gown only served to accent her beauty. The fringe of a thin scarf, blood red, was wrapped in layers around her throat and flowed away into the darkness.

She beckoned soundlessly and I seemed to float above the bubbles and over to a circle of deck chairs. Amanda, Jeanette, Myrtle, and Martha sat in the circle. When Starr approached, they drew in, their heads closing together like petals on a rose at sunset, like a Georgia O'Keeffe painting.

Starr did not stop but beckoned again and I was drawn, against my will, into a darkened corridor. Marsalis's notes had faded now and a piano came in. Ozzie. It had to be him. No one else was able to move his fingers down those keys in quite the same way. Starr paused, listening, then a light came on and she turned in a pirouette. Her gown swirled around her like a parachute and I drew back in shock.

Her ankles were swollen and the veins had collapsed. Her legs were dotted with punctures that resembled the tooth marks of rodents. I backed up, screaming, from the sight but the deck began to shift and I staggered, missing the pool by inches.

The light blinked, went out, and came on again. I looked back to see Starr massaging the veins in her legs. The light went out completely and I scrambled to find my way, running from her voice rushing at me in the dark.

Mali. You know who did this?

Did what?

This thing. This awful thing. I can't sing. Do you know who—?

We were on the top deck now, but the water was still churning around our feet. And there was Tad working his camera, frowning as if he hadn't angled it correctly. Starr's voice faded to an echo and Tad seemed angry because I had interrupted something.

In the morning another hot bath, this time filled with pine salts, eased most of the pain and I was able to leave the house despite Dad's protests. Last night when Tad called I wasn't ready to talk. I let the machine kick in. I'll call him later. Right now I needed to see Jo Jo.

I got off to a late start and it was twelve noon when I arrived at the store. Charleston had been open for two hours and Jo Jo was already making deliveries.

"When it get too hot to cook," Charleston

said, "that's when I make the real money. Jo Jo left with ten orders."

"But it's only twelve noon," I said. "How could folks eat heavy stuff so early in the day?"

He glared at me, incensed that I would critique the ways of black folks or tell him how to run his business.

"For your information, some people—unlike a certain party with only a part-time job—some folks have been in the fields since the crack of dawn. You know, opening stores, shops, newsstands while the moon's still hangin'. All before this certain party has turned over in her sleep. And since they can't close up and go out to lunch, they order in. Because sometimes they get a little bit hungry around this time."

I kept quiet, knowing that I had blown my chance of finding out where Jo Jo was or what route he had taken. I'd have to try to run into him or come back later when Charleston had cooled down.

"Some people make a profession of gettin' on my nerves," he grumbled.

He slapped a soapy industrial-size sponge on the counter and wiped the surface in a sweeping arc. I had been leaning on the counter and knew it was time to leave when the sponge approached my elbow and did not detour.

"I'm sorry, Charleston. I didn't mean it the way it sounded."

He paused and looked at me. "Well, I know you didn't mean nuthin' by it." He leaned closer. "Say, you lookin' kinda washed out. You all right?"

He resumed his work with the sponge but still scrutinized me.

"Come on, Mali. You my favorite girl. What's goin' on?"

"I ran into some static early this morning."

"What kind?"

"Some thug rolled up on me in my block. Wore a mask . . ."

"What?" Charleston stopped and rested his elbows on the counter. "Masks is for bank jobs, big jobs, Mali. What's goin' on? He get anything? Say anything?"

"He wasn't after my bag. He was after me. Dad wasn't home but when doors and windows up and down the block banged open, he cut out but warned me that 'round one was mine.' "

"Meaning . . . he'll be back."

"I suppose."

"Mali, you got to watch your back. I don't want to lose my favorite customer." He reached under the counter and placed a small brown bag near my hand.

"Take it."

I opened the bag and palmed a pocket-sized canister of mace. "Charleston, you probably have a whole arsenal under there."

He shrugged. "Maybe. Maybe not. Anyway, this'll work for you." I dropped it in my purse wondering how effective it would be if I was grabbed from behind again.

Outside, I checked my watch. Jo Jo had left at least forty-five minutes earlier. He could be anywhere, even Washington Heights for all I knew. Running into him would probably be a matter of luck.

Nevertheless, to take my mind off last night's incident, I started walking, doing my usual zigzag between the blocks.

On Powell Boulevard, I spotted the bike chained to a parking meter in front of a beauty parlor on 129th Street. There was only one bike like that in Harlem because Jo Jo had customized it the way some folks redo their cars. It was painted black, red, and green with streaks of silver squiggling through the black. A huge spotlight mounted in the middle of the handlebars dwarfed the two lights on each side. The seat was covered in white sheepskin and the rear fender held a large metal crate with a lid secured by two of the largest locks I had ever seen.

I was admiring his handiwork when he emerged from the store. He stopped when he saw me.

"Hi," I said as he approached the bike and unchained it. "Charleston said you were making the rounds and I'm glad I ran into you. I need to ask you something about someone—"

"Miss Mali, you want to talk, meet me later at 116th Street, somewhere near the mosque. I'll be waitin' there around nine tonight."

With that, he rode off and did not look back.

I continued to walk downtown and at the corner of 124th Street, Ozzie's block, the mailman was filling his sack from the green distribution receptacle. I watched him shoulder the bag, then followed a few paces behind as he moved from house to house. Before he reached the brownstone I fell in step beside him.

"I'm trying to catch up with Ozzie Hendrix," I said, smiling, "but I think he's—"

"You some kind of reporter?" He peered at me, squinty-eyed under his postal service visor.

"No, I—"

" 'Cause if you are, I'm here to tell you the brother wants to be left the hell alone. What happened to his daughter is a damn shame and the cops ain't done shit. I see him every day and I can tell you the man is goin' downhill fast!"

He was like a guard dog ready to sink his incisors into the ankle of any trespasser.

"I—you're right," I said, stepping back. I'm not a reporter. Ozzie is my dad's piano man. At the Club Harlem."

"What?" He stopped and looked at me. "Jeffrey Anderson?"

"Yes, I—"

"How come he ain't lookin' out for his man? How come he ain't stepped to the plate? The brother needs some first aid!"

Before I could think of a sensible answer, he turned on his heel to make his way inside Ozzie's gate, stuff a packet of envelopes and magazines into the empty mailbox, and move on to the next house.

I did not wait to see if a hand would reach between the gate's iron spikes and retrieve the letters; I simply turned away, wanting to cry.

Ozzie was home, but not in good shape.

At the corner again, I found a phone but as usual in an emergency, the damned thing was out of order. Maybe it *was* time to get with the millennium and invest in a cell or a pager or some such high-tech gadget. Every other brother and his mother had one growing out of their ear. I wouldn't be surprised if dogs and cats started wearing cell collars. The owners could let them out for a brisk walk, then when it was time to return, just dial-a-dog. Or call-a-cat.

I detested the idea of being tracked, of being on call, of having a shrill ring interrupt when I'm sitting in the park lost in the rhythm of the birdsong.

To hell with all this rationalizing. It was easier to rush home.

Dad was sitting at the piano going over some sheet music when I walked in. He put his pencil down and I could see tension weigh in as I spoke. His brow wrinkled and his shoulders seemed to sag even lower. Even his voice sounded hopeless. "You didn't ring his bell, did you?"

"No. I thought you'd want to—"

He held up his hand. "I do, but how? Whatever reason he has for going into hibernation I think goes far beyond Starr's death."

"How long are you going to wait before—?"

He shrugged. "Don't know. I'll call again tonight. Drop a word on the machine. Nothing too deep. Just hello and let 'im know we all miss 'im and we're pullin' for 'im. That's all."

That's not enough, I thought. That's not enough.

Upstairs, I listened to the messages: my unit supervisor wanting me to come in in the morning. I was not scheduled but she needed a fill in for someone out ill.

The next message clicked on and Tad's voice, loud and frantic, filled the room: "Mali? I just saw the report. What happened? Why didn't you call me? Are you there?" A second of silence followed and the machine clicked off. I grabbed the receiver intending to call, to let him know I was all right, but the doorbell rang and I knew it was him.

When I opened the door, he looked at me. Then his gaze softened and I heard the light exhalation. "You all right?"

His voice was like a whisper and I wanted to feel his arms around me. He read my mind, reached out, and pulled me to him. "Baby, baby. What happened?"

We remained like that until Dad's footsteps sounded on the stairs, then we sat on the sofa watching as Dad paced the floor. "Can you imagine? The man had on a mask. He wore a ski mask!"

I could feel Tad's eyes on me, as if inspecting for fractures. "The incident report didn't have too many details. What happened, Mali?"

I went over the event and, because Dad was present, omitted the man's parting words. I'd tell that part later, when Dad had gone back downstairs. But a half hour later Dad was still talking.

"You need to be home at a decent hour. No need to be running around town in the middle of the night."

"He's right, Mali. Two-thirty A.M. is kind of late. How come you didn't take a cab? Or call me? I would've picked you up."

I felt his arm resting on my shoulder, his voice soft and concerned, but heard something else, an unasked question: Why was I out at that hour in the first place?

I listened and felt a sudden irritation. I was the victim, not the perp, and didn't appreciate the interrogation. I knew Dad was motivated by fright, by Starr's death. I imagined his blood pressure rising along with his voice. To ask him to calm down was useless.

"Listen," I whispered, "I know you two are upset. So am I. From now on, I'll try to be more alert, watch my back."

But Tad wouldn't let it lay. "All the alertness in the world won't help if you're out at that hour. You're fair game. You need to be home in your house."

I turned to look at him and wondered if he was advising me or an errant child. He brought his hand up and his fingers brushed the back of my neck and then the lobe of my ear. My irritation ebbed, replaced by something else.

"You gotta be careful," he whispered.

So do you, I wanted to say, but Dad was present. I remained quiet, leaned against his shoulder, and felt an exquisite tension build under the light touch of his fingers.

"Promise me next time that you'll call. I'll pick you up from anywhere."

I glanced at him and at that moment I would have promised to walk on the moon. Things were getting a bit thick so I removed myself from the sofa and offered to fix coffee. Dad declined. "I got work to do," he said and retreated back downstairs.

Tad also shook his head. "Gotta get back. You sure you're all right?"

"Never felt better," I whispered.

"Good. No more night owl rambling, okay?"

His kiss came so quickly, I didn't have a chance to agree or not.

Then he was gone.

17

So now it was evening and I had to meet Jo Jo. I waited until Dad left for the club before stepping out. I felt like a kid sneaking off to a forbidden rendezvous. If I hurried, I could be back before midnight. I thought of Cinderella and *her* curfew and decided it was all bullshit. I'd take as long as it took to get what I needed.

At 116th Street, Jo Jo, who had been leaning against a lamppost, fell in step beside me when

I approached. He guided his bike with one hand and the wheels made a slight clicking noise as we walked.

The air was cooler but a sultriness lingered and the street was busy. An evening program had just concluded at Canaan Baptist Church and the sidewalk was teeming with parishioners. Jo Jo guided the bike slowly around them and we moved on, passing a succession of crowded African restaurants. The doors were open to the street and the sound of "Soukouss," a popular West African song, spilled out over the noise and laughter.

On Powell Boulevard we turned north. I glanced at the high wrought iron that enclosed Graham Court, where Zora Neale Hurston once lived. I walked slowly, waiting for Jo Jo to say something. Finally he said, "Charleston told me what happened. You all right?"

"I'm all right," I said. "I'm trying to find someone you might know."

"I figured that. When I saw you earlier, I didn't know if it was a good idea to conversate just then. Sometimes folks get funny if they think you eyein' 'em or tellin' they business. I mean, I see a lot when I'm on these runs but I keep my tongue in my mouth and my mouth shut. Charleston say, 'Better cool than a fool. See, and don't say, and everything will be all right.' "

I smiled at Charleston's advice. Always taut, tight, and straight to the point. As we walked, I saw that although Jo Jo was as tall as I, he was thin as a rail. If I didn't know better, I'd wonder when he'd had his last full meal. But I knew he ate well and probably worked it off with the bike.

"Charleston said you're into rap," I said. "How're you doing?"

"Not bad. Not bad. Want to hear my latest?"

"Why not?" I said, hoping I wasn't going to be weighed down with lyrics glorifying those *B* and *N* words. At the first breath, I'd have to stop him cold. And I'd have to lose whatever chance I had of finding out about the Saturday woman.

"Why not?" I said again.

He started to snap the fingers of his free hand, opening the beat, and the words came out in a singular, acerbic rhythm.

"...Downtown clown
runnin' all around
tellin' everybody
that crime is down
crime is down
he a liar
should be fired
open up your eyes
be surprise
people on the street
with nuthin' to eat
got no bed to
rest they head
that's how it be
but he can't see
crime ain't down
it still around
he a liar
oughta be fired."

I saw the flare in his eyes. He was caught up in the recitation and had to breathe hard to come down, but a minute later, he flashed a smile. "It ain't finished yet. But how you like it so far?"

"Pretty good. I think it's the best I've heard in a long time, Jo Jo. The best one."

The smile faded and he turned serious again. "You know, I wrote that for my friend."

"What does he think of it?"

"It's a she. She ain't heard it yet."

At 125th Street, he held his hand out, pointing toward the west. "She sick. And I can't get her to go to the hospital. I was wonderin' if you could talk to her; bein' that you a woman, she might listen to a woman . . . and bein' that you work in the hospital, doin' the work you do. You know what I'm sayin'?"

"Where does she live?"

He hesitated then said, "I'll have to take you there."

We veered west on 125th Street, passing Showman's Bar, which was crowded with folks celebrating "retirees night." Every seat was taken, the music from the jukebox was blasting, and the windows appeared frosted with air-conditioned excitement.

We passed a string of bodegas, brightly lit hairdressers and nail salons. Folks lounged curbside in plastic beach chairs drinking beer. A ball game boomed from king-size portables and cries of support rose on the night air. "C'mon, whatcha gonna do? Already in the fifth and ain't done nuthin'."

I listened as Jo Jo spoke of the woman we were going to see.

"She was real pretty. Really somethin' to see. I used to deliver to her place all the time. She'd come to the door dressed in those nice evening robes or dresses and she had a perfume that smelled real good. Her hair was done up in those blond wigs and she was always laughing, you know. Like she was on top of the world. She usually had a champagne glass in her hand and her tips were heavy enough to keep me happy for a whole week."

"What's her name?"

"I don't know. Never knew her real name. They called her Saturday 'cause that was her day off. I mean she must've made a pile of cash 'cause she always dressed in the best. Lived in a brownstone near Garvey Park."

Saturday. Sara Lee Brown. She was alive. Sick but still alive. I tried to keep the excitement out of my voice.

"Did she live alone?"

"Naw. Lived with that player just got iced. But she was outta there long before he got killed. I think he put her out when she got too sick to work."

At Broadway, the steel framework of the IRT elevated-train line curved overhead in a skeletal arc. The corners on the far side of the street shone with neon carnival banners of Taco Bell, KFC, and McDonald's.

Beyond that, near the river's edge, stood the peeling, gray-steel girders of that stretch of West Side Highway that Robert Moses, in his heyday as the city's master builder, had left devoid of architectural amenities because, he had determined, it passed through "the colored section."

"Gotta make a detour here," Jo Jo said.

On Broadway, we walked three blocks south to Obaa Koryoe, a large and elegant, candle-lit, Ghanaian restaurant near LaSalle Place. Jo Jo pored over the menu and decided on a take-out order of peanut soup, and a large dish of fried plantains and baked fish with jollof rice.

"Saturday get tired of Charleston's menu so I try to change up from time to time. She like that."

"How did you find her?"

"Just lucky. Harlem ain't that big, you know. One day I was bikin' by and saw this sister diggin' in one of the Dumpsters behind KFC. I went over to drop some coins on her, 'cause, you know, I was in that same situation myself once upon a time and if it wasn't for Charleston, I'd be dead by now. So I never forget. Some days I give up my last nickel."

He dug into his leather fanny pack, extracted a fistful of quarters and stacked them carefully on the counter. He brought out more as the clerk tallied the bill.

We collected the packages and walked back to 125th Street. The lights of a full-service gas station faded in the background as we passed a row of anonymous steel-shuttered buildings. We veered off from the Cotton Club, closed for the night, and walked in the thick darkness of the underside of the West Side Highway, past a club called Harlem Heat Wave, strangely located in an otherwise completely deserted area and lit like a beacon.

Jo Jo slowed down. We approached a row of shuttered garages and auto repair shops which slowly declined into a string of abandoned walk-in storage bins. One bin, larger than the rest, had a corrugated roof and a rusted door held tightly in place from the inside by a loop of wire. The wind blowing off the river carried the faint odor of raw sewage.

He motioned for me to wait. I stepped back as he approached the door with the packages and knocked softly. I didn't hear anything from inside, but he must have because he called out, "It's me. Jo Jo. I got somebody with me."

Another, longer pause and he said, "Can we come in?"

The wire was drawn through the hole and slowly disappeared inside and the door was pushed open. Jo Jo laid his bike against the side of the wall away from the street and motioned for me to stand by his side. He stooped his head and I followed him into a small, airless space lit by an oil lamp. A kerosene heater was situated just inside the door, unlit, but the scent of the oil saturated everything.

"This my friend Mali," Jo Jo said, setting the packages down on a legless table that rested on a small crate.

"Hello," I said, gazing at Sara Lee Brown seated on a low stool. Tuesday had told me that Sara was in her mid-thirties but she appeared a lot older. Despite the weather, she was dressed in layers of clothing—a dress, a sweater, a coat, several pairs of socks, and a pair of men's shoes. Shadows danced on the walls as she reached out to shake my outstretched hand.

"How you doin', Mali? Jo Jo, don't tell me you went and finally got yourself a girlfriend. I don't believe it."

When she smiled, I was surprised to see a full set of teeth, hers or someone else's, but a full set nonetheless. Her thin face was a mask of fine lines, probably from dehydration, and her hair was covered by a print scarf knotted at the back of her neck. She had a dry cough and reached for a handkerchief to cover her mouth when she felt one coming on.

"We brought you something," Jo Jo said. He opened the packages and for a minute, the mélange of African spices filled the space and chased the odor of the kerosene.

"This peanut soup'll do you good," he said, speaking softly as to a child reluctant to take its medicine. The spices worked their magic and in five minutes, the container was empty and she got started on the plate of fish, plantains, and rice.

I looked around in the flickering light at the crates piled against the walls and at the bedroll that rested on a length of board atop a broken metal frame. The floor was covered with pieces of discarded carpet, and carpet padding was tacked to the walls. Old cushions, flat and stained, were stacked near the makeshift bed and a padlocked metal trunk, which probably contained all her worldly possessions, stood nearby.

I was not going to get the story from her, not tonight at least. Probably not ever. She looked extremely frail and I imagined that whatever was wrong with her had probably cut into Short Change's profits, so he had kicked her to the curb. From there, the Technicolor dream had evaporated, the blond wigs disappeared, and her life fell into a nightmare of living a week here, a week there, anywhere she had been welcomed. Sometimes, only for a night.

Then when the novelty of her presence had been eclipsed by other realities, she had been shown the door by a string of well-meaning hosts who strung out the apologies:

Sara, I got husbands/boyfriends/bills/kids/mouths to feed/things to do/etc., etc. You can understand where I'm comin' from, can't you?

And she had nodded and smiled, always smiled because maybe she might be able to return one day when she came across a few dollars or some other miracle.

And so this place beckoned. Cold and damp and dirty but where no one was likely to come up with those apologies.

Sara Lee ate noisily, as if she was accustomed to eating alone and needed sound to keep her company. I had her story, most of it anyway, and she didn't have to say a word.

"I know what you thinkin'," she said. She had glanced up before I had a chance to look away. "Life ain't always been like this. At one time I was a high flyer. So far up there and so into the money that nobody could come close to what I made."

I glanced around the space crowded with the detritus of another life. I wanted Jo Jo to say something but he too was silent and seemed awed by how fast she had eaten. In less than ten minutes all the plates and containers were empty and now we sat silent in the dim glow.

"Uh, Saturday, we were . . . I mean, I was wonderin' if you changed your mind about goin' to see a doctor, or maybe to a clinic."

She looked from him to me and back again.

"With what? I told you before, it cost dollars even to walk across the street these days, let alone walk into a clinic."

She turned to me then, looking at my clothes, shoes, haircut, and the resentment at where life had brought her welled up but didn't spill over as I had expected. Instead, tears came. "I'd like to get outta here. God knows this ain't no way to live. One more week in this dirty place and I'll be dead. If it wasn't for Jo Jo . . ."

Her voice was barely audible although we sat almost shoulder to shoulder in the small enclosure.

"He used to deliver to me in the old days," she said, nodding to him. "I was in a brownstone. Livin' good. Very good. But things happened. I wasn't as careful as I shoulda been. Now I'm sick as a dog. Probably won't see another year . . ."

I thought of Monday, Tuesday, Thursday, Friday, and the stuff that had happened in their lives—abuse, neglect, rape, the desperate need for love, for money; getting messed up by the wrong promise from the wrong man. Whatever it was that had brought them to this life, in one way or another, they had managed to survive.

But Sara Lee had left before S.C. had been killed. I wanted to ask how long she'd been living here but I kept quiet. With no walls to hang a calendar, time for the hungry is measured by the next meal, the way time for an addict is measured by the next fix.

The difference was that Sara Lee had probably had a major falling-out with Short Change. Maybe she was angry enough to even the score? I stole another glance at her in the dim light and at the appalling surroundings. I imagined the makeshift roof leaking in a storm, or collapsing under the weight of snow in winter; the door trembling against the wind from the river.

Saturday, who was accustomed to fine lingerie and bed linen, now slept in an overcoat and when the temperature dropped, woke up with numb toes and fingers. I imagined her trying to wash up in the public bathroom of the fast food restaurants on the corner. How often had they chased her away?

I glanced at her again and saw the flat look of resignation. "Sara Lee, would you go to the hospital if we take you?"

"You know this ain't no way for you to live," Jo Jo chimed in, backing me up. "Couple months you be dead."

Sara looked around, appraising her habitat. Jo Jo followed her gaze. "Remember how you used to live?" he asked softly.

"I was well then," she murmured. "Young and healthy and everybody said I was pretty. Everybody."

"And you were," he said. "I remember how you were. So you gonna let us—"

"What about my things? This is all I—"

"Don't worry about them," I said. "We'll take care of all that after we get you settled, okay?"

That seemed to satisfy her and I said, "I'll stay with you while Jo Jo finds a cab."

"Why not an ambulance?" he asked.

"If we call an ambulance," I said, "they'll take her to the nearest hospital in the area and if she has no coverage, they'll probably treat her and release her. Or worse, not treat her at all. Since I work at Harlem Hospital, I can cut through some tape and arrange a few things, especially long-term care once she's discharged. And I don't mean discharged to one of those shelters either."

Sara Lee looked at me and the skin on her drawn face seemed to take on color in the flickering light. "You bein' for real?"

"Yes, I am," I said.

18

As the old folks used to say, especially if they had just missed hitting the number by one digit, "If it wasn't for bad luck, I wouldn't have no damn luck at all."

It turned out that the Saturday woman was HIV positive, which I suspected. The dry cough had been a symptom of tuberculosis, which I had not suspected. This called for tuberculosis testing for everyone who had been in touch with her and everyone who had been in touch with those who had been in touch.

Jo Jo had to take off from his lucrative delivery job to await results. Charleston was philosophical about the loss of business as he too went to be tested. "Shit happens" was all he said. Dad had to be tested and so did I.

And of course when I saw Lieutenant Tad Honeywell, dedicated, hardworking member in good standing with the NYPD—even though officers were tested regularly and received booster shots, and even though I had not been in close, physical contact with him since I'd visited the Saturday woman—I felt bound to tell him of the situation. (Harlem being a small place and the Capitol of Communication, where the drums worked overtime, he would've heard the word soon anyway.)

We had gotten Sara Lee to the hospital Friday and the following Monday evening, when Tad stopped by to see me, I had the not-so-pleasant experience of watching his eyebrows scrunch up, his lips flatten into a straight line. And as best I could, I tried to ignore the ominous throat-clearing sounds as if he were gearing up for a speech before a joint session of Congress.

Actually, it was his eyes that did it. It was his eyes. The warmth drained away and glaciers seemed to form around the irises. The look was more effective than any words he could have mustered.

I should've felt chastened, or something, but I didn't. I couldn't. I knew I had done the right thing and that, I thought defensively, was that.

We sat in the living room, he on the sofa and me in the chair facing him, listening to the intermittent sounds of Dad's bass floating up from his studio. A recording of a piano solo by Ozzie accompanied him, filling in the space. Over the weekend Dad had called several times before Ozzie had finally picked up the phone late Sunday night. Few words were exchanged and Ozzie had said that that was the way he wanted it.

He had hung a DO NOT DISTURB sign on himself, the same way

Chrissie had done aboard ship, except Ozzie had a real tragedy to deal with. Chrissie had only her smart-ass self.

"Can I offer you something to drink?" I said, surprised at the calm formality of my invitation. I gazed at his profile, watched his brows unknit slightly even though the jaw muscles remained tight enough to bend steel. He mumbled something, a sound which I loosely interpreted to mean yes, and I went to the bar to fix a Walker and water for him and an Absolut and orange for myself (double shot to calm my one last nerve).

This time when I returned to the sofa, I sat beside him, but minutes later we were still sipping in silence. At least I was.

"Mali," he finally whispered, the traces of anger gone but replaced by something I couldn't name. "Mali, I don't know how else to impress upon you, to make you understand the danger you place yourself in, when you . . ."

I listened quietly, I really did, but he must have seen something in my expression when he caught my glance. A look that said, "Yes, yes, I hear, I understand, but you know how I am and that's why—partly why—you love me, right? Am I right?"

No answer because I couldn't ask. As angry as he was, I wasn't about to step out on that particular limb. He might have surprised me with an answer I didn't want to hear.

In the silence, I listened to the clink of ice cubes falling together as he shifted the glass from one hand to the other. And I heard the sound of irritation as he drew in a deep breath.

Finally (and formally), he placed the glass on the low table next to the package he had brought and rose from the sofa with military precision. I remained seated and looked up to gaze at a stranger, someone I'd never seen before.

"I'll be seeing you," he said evenly.

I remained on the sofa as if I'd been planted and I did not look around, even when the door slammed shut behind him.

Well, I thought. And thought some more. What to do? I sat there for several minutes waiting for the sound of the bell. So I could run to the door and hear him say, "I forgot something." And I'd say, "Oh. Your package." And he'd say, "No. Not that. I forgot this." And he'd look long and hard and would melt and I'd step close, close, the extraordinary vision of him blurred by tears of repentance and passion, and I'd feel his arms slip to my waist and his mouth begin to explore the curve of my neck and finally my mouth would open in a deep breath and . . .

But there was no bell, dammit! He was gone. I sat there staring at his drink, barely touched. And at my own glass, as clean as if I had washed it. Even the ice cubes were gone. I glanced at the unopened package on the table near his glass. These were the pictures we had taken on the cruise, pictures that we were supposed to look at and maybe laugh over together.

The packet was thick, probably held about a hundred photos because we had snapped and clicked and flashed and posed and smiled and vogued the entire seven days. Pictures port, starboard, fore, and aft. Pictures in the Chart Room, with its concert-grand pedal harp, and snapshots of the two of us seated at the Chappell grand piano, an impressive walnut antique that had once graced the ballroom of the RMS *Queen Mary* and was probably worth more than the *QE2* itself. In the 1950s, the piano had been stolen. This huge piano, which weighed close to a thousand pounds, had simply vanished when the ship was docked in New York. It had taken twenty years to recover it, traced by its serial number to a secondhand shop in Chelsea.

I stared at the packet, trying to imagine other scenes and bits of information without disturbing the wrapping. The minute we'd returned to New York, Tad had put the film in the shop and we had planned to reminisce about those good times and plan for more.

Maybe I should wait, not look at them until he comes back, then we can share the memories . . .

Share what??

It was Mama's voice. Just when I needed to hear her.

Girl, if you're waiting to exhale, you'll die of respiratory failure. Didn't I teach you anything? Open up that package. Give you something to do besides sitting there moaning and groaning like an old woman. And even old women don't do that nowadays. All that is definitely not healthy. Get yourself together and get real. So the man's angry, upset, hurt, provoked, offended. So what. Too bad. He shouldn't be surprised at anything you do and you shouldn't be surprised that he's angry. You know him as well as he knows—thinks he knows—you. Come on. I raised a better child than this.

And so you did, Mama. So you did.

I broke the tape on the package, turned it upside down and the packets slid out. I opened the first envelope and stared at the photo of Chrissie posing in front of her cabin door, one hand on the knob and the other on her hip. I flipped to the next photo and there she was again, smiling her tacky smile straight into the camera. The phone rang as I was about to shred the pictures and I snatched the receiver from the cradle.

"Well?"

"Well, my goodness, girl. Do I have the right number or are you not accepting unsolicited calls this evening?"

"Elizabeth?"

"Yes. Should I hang up and try again?"

"No. No. But I'm damned pissing fighting mad," I said.

"I can hear that. Come on down to Perk's and talk about it. I'm sitting at the bar."

Through my own anger, I heard the strain in her voice. "Elizabeth, what's going on with you? Are you all right?"

"I'm not sure."

"What's the matter?"

"Travis has been arrested."

19

I called downstairs to Dad, stuffed the photos into my shoulder bag, and quickly left the house. Ten minutes of fast walking brought me to 123rd Street and Manhattan Avenue, where the soft lights of Perk's Restaurant spilled out over the corner. Inside, the even softer seats made the place a welcome watering spot for the weary.

As I approached, my mind fastened on Ozzie holed up inside his home just around the corner. Although Dad had spoken to him, he still had not seen him. Friday, he had hoped up until the very last minute that Ozzie would pull himself out of the house and maybe show at the club but it didn't happen.

The piano man from Brooklyn, who loved jazz, was happy to sit in once again and the crowd, Dad said, had loved him.

But Ozzie was absent and I knew how Dad felt. Now Travis had been arrested.

I stepped into Perk's and the bar area was crowded—young rising stars of industry, finance, and other professions were there as were the usual crew of fishers and anglers out to get their hooks into a suitable specimen. And, as at most gatherings, there were the players and trollers, interested only in the catch of the day.

The crowd was cool: the women threaded to the nines in Versace with add-on hair, nails, and contacts, and gazing with slightly bored, Mona Lisa smiles into the pink glow of the mirror behind the bar. The truly bored—those with no prospects—were frowning hard enough to embed a permanent wrinkle in their foreheads.

The guys, even cooler, raised brandy snifters with studied nonchalance, and all were listening to the latest sound of Silk.

I scanned the buffed and polished lineup then spied Elizabeth seated at a small table near the window.

She gathered her purse and her glass and we walked down the short flight of steps to the dining room.

"So what happened?" I asked once we were seated and the waiter had disappeared to fill our order. I spoke low, aware of the proximity of the other diners.

Elizabeth leaned forward. "I thought Honeywell would have told you already. The police traced the weapon that killed that pimp, Henry Stovall—Short Change. It belonged to Travis. Now they're trying to say that Travis also killed Starr. You know, wrap it neatly and close both cases."

"What's the motive?"

"Something easy. Jealousy."

I nodded, thinking of my close encounter with Chrissie Morgan, thinking of those damn pictures contaminating my purse, and thinking how delicious it would feel to press my fingers into that chicken-wattled throat and to shred that weave until her bald scalp gleamed in the sun. . . .

"Mali?"

"What?"

Elizabeth reached across the table and tapped my hand. "Okay, we'll get back to Travis. Tell me what's eating you."

I was too angry to speak so I pulled out the photos and spread them before her like a losing hand in a poker game. Elizabeth looked from me to the pictures and back again. "Where'd you get these? This is Travis's wife."

"So it is," I murmured. "It seems that Tad was quite busy with his camera on the cruise. And the woman came on to him as if I wasn't even there. He hasn't seen these yet, but we got into a little misunderstanding about a half hour ago and he walked out. That man actually walked out. Now I wonder—"

Elizabeth held up her hand. "Don't even go there, girl."

"Too late. I already went. And words were exchanged. Jealousy," I said, "is a damn dangerous thing."

The waiter returned with the drinks and despite my earlier indulgence, I had no trouble appreciating the subtle, soothing smoothness of this new round.

"Jealousy," Elizabeth said, stirring a Madras—a concoction of vodka, orange and cranberry juice on the rocks—"is only dangerous when you act on it incorrectly."

"Well, hell. What else does one do?"

"One plans," Elizabeth said. "One organizes, strategizes, optimizes."

"What are you getting at?"

"I mean, you look at the situation and figure out how the hell you gonna kick the bitch's ass."

"Elizabeth!"

"With the least repercussions, of course."

She raised her glass to her mouth and I watched in suprise as my friend—respected attorney, pillar of the community, member of her church's usher board, and assistant Girl Scout leader, who spent much of her spare time lecturing in local schools about the power of proper language—was now expressing herself most improperly.

"I don't believe I heard you correctly," I said.

"I know. I know. I wanted to get a rise out of you. And the situation doesn't call for that long face. Wait a few days, Mali. Then call him, tell him you'd like to talk about whatever it is that's coming between you two."

She flipped one of Chrissie's snapshots and studied it closely. "I certainly don't believe this over-the-hill potential butterball is even in your league. So, what ticked him off?"

"My usual nosiness," I sighed. "Remember a few years ago when the tour director of the Uptown Children's Chorus was killed? I was told to let the police handle the investigation, not to interfere. But Erskin Harding was my friend. I saw him murdered. I had to do something.

"And I felt the same about Thea, the barmaid killed in that alley behind the Half Moon Bar. All the signs pointed to Bert's brother, Kendrick, remember?

"Now with this latest incident, Tad warned me once again to mind my own business, that they'd look for Ozzie. Well, I'm glad they didn't find him. He's holed up in his house, you know."

"Probably never really looked for him. They got Travis instead."

"Meanwhile Ozzie's deteriorated to the point where he's completely isolated himself, and probably battling a deep depression. Dad has no idea what to do and he's not in very good shape himself. I'm not sticking my nose in everyone's business, just trying to figure out how to help Ozzie. But I've drawn a blank. I've been in and out of Short Change's stable, spoken to most of his women, and I'm still no closer than I was on day one. Now they've arrested Travis?"

"Well, I'll tell you this off the record," Elizabeth said, picking up one picture and then another to study. "Travis's wife is a real piece of work. He's her third hubby and she's fighting like hell to hold on to him. He's a few years younger than she and she probably feels this is her last go 'round."

"If she's fighting so hard to hold on to her husband, why was she coming on to another man, specifically my man?"

"It's psychological, I guess. If a person is losing on one front, sometimes they focus on another just to prove to themselves that they still have what it takes. All of us want to feel attractive, Mali. All of us. Sometimes, when a man looks at a woman, some days she will settle just for a smile. Other times, if bad things are happening in her life, she mistakes that smile for something else, for a declaration of love.

"Now with Tad, I can understand Chrissie and a whole lot of women zoning in. I mean, what do you expect? Look at that bod and that beautiful skin. And need I mention his hair—all edged in silver while every other man his age is losing theirs? Don't tell me he wasn't the best-looking brother on the boat."

"Listen, Elizabeth, you've known me for a long time, ever since we were kids—and during that time, you know I have never gone to war over any man. A few days ago, only a stroke of luck saved her sorry soul."

Elizabeth sighed, returning Chrissie's picture to the pile on the table. "You know, what I see is a woman who should have appreciated her husband for who he was instead of what he had. Instead, she drained Travis dry. You should see the financial albatross the guy has hanging on him. Bills that would make Trump's babes blush. Saks, Bloomie's, Bergdorf's, Versace. She's practically on a first-name basis with most of the boutiques on Mad Ave."

"What about Travis's relationship with Starr? Could some of those bills have come from her?"

"Not unless she signed Wifey's name on those slips. And so far all the signatures look alike to me. Simply put, Wifey is afflicted with a severe case of credit card–itis."

The waiter returned with a tray of a half dozen appetizers, which we had ordered in lieu of entrées. Everything looked good but it took major effort for me to lift a fork.

"Do you think Travis did it?"

"Did what?" Elizabeth glanced up from her plate. She may have had a setback but her appetite was still intact.

"Do you think he—"

"—I don't know, Mali. I can't talk about that."

I returned the pictures to my purse, then concentrated on Tina Turner's crackling lyrics pulsing through the hum of conversation. My thoughts focused on Tad as I listened.

"You've barely touched your plate," Elizabeth said.

"I'm not hungry," I said, trying to block out the wail of "Steamy Windows." Tad loved Tina's music, said every time he heard her voice, he closed his eyes and saw my legs moving. High heels, black stockings with rhinestone-studded seams. The man had imagination.

Snap out of it, girl. Dreaming won't do anything but give you heartburn.

"You're right, Mama."

Elizabeth looked up. "What?"

"Nothing," I said, looking at my watch. "What do you say we take a walk over to Bert's place. See what's going on."

As in other neighborhoods, the beauty business in Harlem has its slow days and most shops, hopeful of walk-ins, remained open with bright lights blazing and television blaring even if all the chairs remained empty. We stood outside Bertha's closed shop and shook our heads.

"It's not even that late," Elizabeth said, checking her watch. "Maybe we should've called first."

The shop was dark except for the dim light illuminating the spiral stair in the rear that led up to Bert's apartment. Next door to the shop, the entrance which led to the other apartment and accessed her own place was locked. I thought about ringing the bell when the door opened and Bert stopped in surprise when she saw us.

"Girl! I just called you. Left a message on your machine. Y'all got to come with me."

"What happened?"

"Tell you as we movin'," she said as she stepped into the street and held out her hand. When the cab stopped, we piled in and she gave the driver an address on 148th Street near Frederick Douglass Boulevard.

"And I want you to drive like a life depended on it," she said.

The cabbie turned to face her with a worried smile. "One of you sisters pregnant?"

"No!" Bert snapped. "And if we were, it ain't none a' your business."

"Okay. Okay. Just asking. Just need to know how soon you—"

"Look, just get us where we got to go, please."

"Yes, ma'am," he whispered, thinking of the tip he might have already talked himself out of.

"So what's going on?" I spoke low enough to exclude the driver, whose ears seemed to grow like antennas.

"Would you believe it, it's Franklin's mama. I mean it's Franklin—"

"What happened?" Elizabeth asked.

"Well, you know he got a touch a' diabetes, which he's been controllin' with diet, but lately he been havin' some dizziness. He went to the doc and he was put in the hospital right away for tests. Went in yesterday and wasn't supposed to complete everything for another few days.

"Well, wouldn't you know his mama called me a few minutes ago, like to given me heart failure when I hear her cryin'. Woman said she heard the key in her door and then who's standing there at the foot of her bed but Franklin. Nearly scared the shit out of her and she an old lady too."

"Maybe they completed the tests and released him early," I said. "Maybe he wanted to surprise her."

"Surprise, hell. He nearly stopped her heart. So when I got on the phone, he's all apologetic, sayin' he was worried about her and had to see how she was doin'. I mean I already told him I'd look after her 'til he get out. And to top it all off, the tests weren't even done yet. They was still preppin' 'im, he said."

"Well, how did he leave the hospital?"

"On his two feet," Bert said. "He just walked out."

"He signed out?"

"Read my fat lips. Walked out. Put on his street clothes over his hospital duds and skipped right on past the nurses' station. His mama's all right so now he wants me to come with him and walk him back in."

"I don't believe it," Elizabeth said.

"I do," Bert said, settling back in the cab. She was still angry but not too angry to talk. "I remember when I was comin' up, there was this lady named Frances, real pretty, lived in the apartment on the top floor, got sick and the ambulance came for her. Took her to Harlem Hospital and they operated on her burst appendix. Her boyfriend and her had just had an argument and broken up. He went back to her apartment to apologize and found out she had gone to the hospital.

"He rushed over to Harlem, where they tell him he couldn't see her. Come back tomorrow. Hell, he couldn't wait. Had to see his sweetie. Walked around to the 137th Street side of the building—I'm talkin' about the old hospital now, not the new one. The old one had those iron fire escapes. Well, he sure climbed them at eleven o'clock that night and snuck in there on the fourth floor and talk about managed care? Didn't he get to see his love before the nurse came in and screamed so loud she woke up the whole damn floor?

"Girl come home a week later, smilin' her head off. Said love, true love, make you do stuff nobody else understand."

"I suppose so," I said, thinking of Tad and how I'd like to climb up his building the way George Willig in 1977 had scaled one of the Twin Towers. He'd tied up traffic for blocks around the World Trade Center and made headlines.

Then I thought of Chrissie and imagined climbing up the side of her building like King Kong at the Empire State except she wasn't Fay Wray and I damn sure wouldn't be doing it for love.

The cabbie pulled up in front of a five-story building on 148th Street and Franklin was waiting on the stoop. He strode down the steps and climbed in the cab as if we were on our way to a party and had stopped by to pick him up to join the fun. He got in the front next to the cabbie and turned to smile at Bert, who by now was not speaking.

"Where to?" the cabbie asked.

Franklin gave the address of the hospital and the cab turned north on Powell Boulevard, sped along the 155th Street viaduct, and turned onto Broadway.

"How's your mother doing?" I asked to break the silence.

"Oh, she's fine," he said, glancing at Bertha. But she neither answered or acknowledged his presence.

Elizabeth stayed in the lobby while the three of us walked to the visitors' station. Franklin asked for a pass to see Franklin Gibson. Bertha signed in and we said nothing as the clerk pulled the large plastic placard from the hook with the room number on it.

We strolled down the corridor to the bank of elevators, stepped off on the eighth floor, and walked past the nurses' station with its multiple banks of monitors, past the patients' lounge with its elaborate display of plants and the wide-screen television, past the chatter of the hospital attendants trundling carts of trays and linens, and finally into his room, where he stepped out of his street clothes.

He reminded me of Superman, who always seemed to have his uniform on underneath. The pajamas had pale stripes and even had a handkerchief pocket.

"I'll see you later, Franklin," I said, and left the room to join Elizabeth. Whatever words Bertha had for Franklin, I'm sure she wanted to deliver in private. I only hoped they wouldn't be too hard or too loud.

Elizabeth was sitting in the lounge when I stepped off the elevator.

"So how did it go?"

"He's in the room. No problem."

Elizabeth shook her head and sighed. "Amazing what some folks will do."

Bert joined us five minutes later. "I was too mad to stay," she said. "I'm goin' back to his mama's place and spend the night."

The trip home was slower. Traffic was backed up on the viaduct and our cab crept along 155th Street past the Masonic Lodge and came to a halt at the corner of St. Nicholas Avenue, where the Fat Man bar once stood.

It had started to rain, a summer rain that always began small with light drops that lulled you into thinking it would last for only a minute, perhaps, and move on, but it got serious, and the drum of water on the cab's roof sounded like a herd of horses.

I thought of the Saturday woman and wondered if the deluge had washed away the roof of the now empty shed that was once her refuge. I was glad I did what I did, no matter what Tad thought. I peered out the window as we inched along the viaduct and through the rain; the traffic down on Eighth Avenue resembled a wavering ribbon of light.

To my left, small square specks of light from the upper floors of the Polo Ground houses loomed like beacons through the mist. The Polo Grounds, the old home of the New York Giants and the New York Mets.

On a good day, Dad swears he can still hear the echo of the crack of Willie Mays's bat.

At the corner of Seventh Avenue where the bridge connected Harlem to the Bronx, a cop arced his flashlight to divert traffic around a minor accident. At 148th Street, we dropped Bertha off at Franklin's mother's house and at 139th Street, I stepped out of the cab and waved good night to Elizabeth. The squeal of the tires died in the rain, and sound and movement were suspended, but somehow, in this quiet I felt I was not alone.

I palmed the mace and glanced over my shoulder as I put my key in the door. Ruffin's bark and his quick movements reassured me and I was glad to be home. I shed my wet clothes, showered, and finally fell into bed and went through a series of meditations. I did not want to dream about Tad or those damn photos.

20

I didn't sleep long. The clock read 3 A.M. Tuesday morning and I'd only gotten about three hours' sleep. For a minute or so, I sat on the edge of the bed listening in the dark to the rain beating against the window. Then I retrieved my notebook from the floor and turned on the small lamp on the night table.

I flipped to page one, the night of Starr's murder, or rather the night we discovered she had been murdered. She had, according to the autopsy, been killed on Saturday, two days before she was found. And her killer, according to the report, had been left-handed or at least ambidextrous and had a hefty build. I guess the medical examiner figured that out from the depth and direction of the wound. Someone hefty and left-handed.

And damned angry, I penciled in the margin.

A large blowup of her picture in the living room had been slashed but the marks were clean. No blood. Had the picture been defaced before Starr was killed or were two different knives used? If it happened before she was killed, had she known the person well enough to allow him into her apartment? Had there been an argument? Had the situation turned ugly?

I read again the notes I'd made of the conversations at Starr's wake, and closed the notebook and went to stand near the window. The rain came down and hit the sidewalk like stones. It bent the leaf-heavy branches of the trees, arrayed like sentries, and the glow of the streetlights shimmered like halos.

I wanted to call someone to talk, to speculate about how a knife wound so deep could have been inflicted without a fight. But Elizabeth would have killed me if I dialed her at this hour. And Tad? Well, he and I couldn't discuss this at all. I could possibly call and apologize and suggest that whatever had made him angry wouldn't happen again, but that would be like easing a Band-Aid over a sore that hadn't been properly cleansed.

I pressed my forehead against the window and felt the chill dampness of the glass, and since I couldn't see anything through the downpour, I closed my eyes and imagined, wished myself back in bed, lying spoon fashion against him. I saw his perfect body—strong arms, long legs, skin smooth and brown against the pale sheet.

And him moving from sleep, not quite awake but like a baby instinctively searching for its mother's milk, searching and finding the curve of my hip and murmuring softly when he touched it.

And me, coming alive at feeling him come alive, and rolling over to submerge myself in a hot, sugared rainfall of middle-of-the-night kisses.

Wake up, girl!

"Ah, Mama, you show up at the damnedest times."

I come when I need to, and don't you forget that.

"You're right and I'm sorry. I didn't mean—"

I know you didn't, baby. Now climb back in bed. Get some real sleep. You got a busy day ahead of you.

I didn't question her. I never did.

I left the window and climbed into bed and, in the silence, allowed Mom's voice to tuck me in.

When I woke, the deluge had moved on and though the sidewalk was still glistening and the leaves still hung wet and heavy, the sun was out and working hard to dry up everything in the eighty-degree warmth. Strivers Row with its orderly line of three-story brownstones and graystones and curtained windows and iron balconies lay suspended in early morning calm.

Walking at dawn always helped to put things in perspective and I needed to make sense of the stuff that had happened. I collared Ruffin and we left the house. On St. Nicholas Avenue, the spires of St. James church caught the early morning glimmer of light and the air was fresh and thick with the wet fragrance of the grass in St. Nicholas Park.

We turned up the hill at 145th Street, passing the Bowery Apartments, where Dinah Washington once lived. At Convent Avenue Baptist Church, the entrance had been blocked off for a funeral and a small crowd had gathered. They held black-edged programs and their wrists moved fast and light as they fanned themselves.

I thought of Starr—gone without a proper send-off. And all the unshed tears were still locked in, taking their toll on Ozzie and on my dad.

I led Ruffin past the John Henrik Clarke House and Hamilton Grange and retraced our steps down the hill bordering the park. St. Nicholas Avenue had now stirred to life and folks stepped out in a steady stream, heading for the subway. By the time I reached home, I had decided what I was going to do but it was no consolation when I saw Dad.

Despite the morning ritual of cool shower and hot coffee, he looked as if sleep had eluded him.

"Alvin called," he said.

"Oh," I said, glad for conversation. "How's he doing?"

"Enjoying himself. Enjoying life. That kid's so lucky."

A simple statement that I tried not to read too much into; tried not to wonder if Dad was looking at Alvin from the perspective of age and all its attendant tragedies.

Yes, I thought. Alvin's lucky but as young as he is, look at what he'd had to live through. Both parents dying in that accident in Europe. People weren't supposed to die while on vacation, Alvin had said. How could something like that happen?

Each time he mentions it, I see my sister's face, smiling as we kiss good-bye at JFK. Alvin and Dad and I waving as she and her husband board the plane for their first vacation in years. And that was the last we saw of them until the bodies were returned, mangled, broken in a hiking accident.

I thought of Tad and despite my simmering resentment, I wanted to kiss him, thank him for having Captain Bo as a friend, a generous man who had welcomed Alvin aboard his four-masted St. Croix schooner at a moment's notice.

"I can swim, hoist a sail, cut bait, even fry the fish I catch," Alvin had said. "Some are funny-looking and have funny names but they taste pretty good."

I wanted to hear his voice again, wavering these days between high squeak when he's really excited then dropping back to the low bass of puberty. Better yet, I wish I could've joined him aboard the schooner. Had I done so, I wouldn't be gritting my teeth over Miss Chrissie and her death-defying circus act around Tad.

I felt my jaw clamping again and a stress headache waiting in the wings so I shut down that part of my brain. It was an effort but I tuned in again to Dad.

"He's gonna call again around eleven tonight. I told him you'd be home."

I juggled my mental calendar and postponed the night stuff. The Lenox Lounge could wait 'til tomorrow. But the other stuff was daytime stuff. That was all right.

"I'll be here. I can't wait to talk to him."

Dad nodded and retreated to his studio and minutes later, the soft melody of an old Oscar Peterson tune drifted upstairs to where I sat nursing a second cup of coffee and envying his ability to fall back into his music for comfort. When I stressed out, I had nothing to fall back on, and that nothingness usually produced unintended consequences.

I took another shower, donned a wrap skirt and sleeveless blouse and at ten o'clock, I was out the door and walking down Powell Boulevard toward 125th Street, where I arrived at Elizabeth's office unannounced. This time I only had to wait a half hour before her conference ended and she escorted an elderly woman to the elevator. Back in the office, she gathered a stack of folders together and placed them in the cabinet.

"How about breakfast? I've been working since sunup."

"Sounds good to me," I said. "I'm always ready to eat."

She locked the door, hung a smiley-face clock outside indicating her return, and we strolled to 132nd Street to Wells Restaurant, where the chicken and waffles revived my body although I still needed to work on my spirit.

"So," Elizabeth said, pouring half a bottle of syrup over her waffles, "you're asking if the cops were looking for a left-handed assailant? Yes, Travis is left-handed, but for that matter, so is his wife. And so are you. So are probably one hundred men, women, and suspicious-looking teenagers within a ten-block radius of this restaurant. And despite the autopsy, the wound could've come from a back slash by a right-handed person."

Elizabeth was handling my lawsuit against NYPD for wrongful dismissal. She works hard for her clients and she has an impressive track record. Her practice is successful, and she lives quite well in a brownstone overlooking the grassy expanse of Marcus Garvey Park. I decided long ago that if I ever got into serious trouble, I'd step over Johnnie Cochran to have her on my side.

"How's Travis doing?" I said.

"Okay. The court agreed that there's no danger of him fleeing; he's a solid businessman with ties to the community, and he'll be out on bail sometime today."

"I'm glad to hear that," I said, wondering how I could get to speak with him. It might be a breach of ethics to ask Elizabeth to set up a meeting. But Harlem is a small place. I'd surely see him one way or another. I needed to know how he felt about Starr. And if he might have had a confrontation with Ozzie. Ozzie was so protective of Starr, he and Travis might've had some words.

We left Wells. Elizabeth returned to the stack of paperwork at her office and I went to see Charleston. When I approached the narrow store, Jo Jo had not yet come in so I felt free to talk, to ask questions about Short Change.

"The man's dead. Why you so interested?"

"That's why I'm interested," I said, leaning on the narrow counter. Charleston turned from me to add more seasoning to two large pots of his secret sauce bubbling on the back burners. He stirred them, replaced the lids, and mopped his face in the heat.

"I don't know that much. Only what I heard. You know what I'm sayin'."

It was his usual disclaimer to ensure that he wouldn't end up on the wrong side of a lawsuit or the business end of someone's weapon.

"Short Change was about forty-something. I don't know if he was born here but he sure grew up here. I mean he was a New Yorker, a Harlemite. Shoulda learned a little somethin' about style. But he musta been color blind or somethin'. Boy dressed in the flashiest, loudest, pimp-style outfits that ever came off the rack. Even when he was growin' up, couldn't stay away from them screamin' jackets. And forget about the pants. You'd a' thought he was one a' them 1940s dudes just stepped off the 'hound from some backwoods tenant farm.

"But that was the way he was. Not much school that I know of. When he was real young, he dropped out to hang out. Musta learned somethin', though, 'cause he sure had the women comin' and goin'. Could run a rap make a grandmama give up her food stamps and smile while she doin' it.

"Heard his mama was a stroller, that's how he got here. Then he disappeared for a while. No jail time 'cause I woulda heard. But when he came back he was pullin' plenty attitude. Said he was gonna be rich before he was thirty and retire before he was forty, and wasn't gonna see a day's work in between.

"Said the money was gonna come to him, he wasn't goin' after it. I mean he talked loud but seem like he made it happen. Some of it, anyway, what with all those women and that big house near Garvey Park."

"If he had so many women, why couldn't he leave Starr alone?" I asked.

"Who knows? Cat had a real bad ego problem. Real bad. Say no to him and he make it seem like a challenge. He used to hang in the Casablanca and set up the bar. The other players was cool, but Short Change was always showin', you know, drawin' a crowd. Had his women paradin' by in next to nuthin' and that see-through stuff. Maybe he needed to make up for how short and lightweight he was. People needed to see him, know he was there and all that. Anyway, he's gone and nobody knows who sent him on his way."

I watched as he pulled a large bag of chickens out of the fridge and placed them in a tub of cool water. Later, he would add the seasoning that caused the long lines to form outside the store.

"Personally," he said, inspecting the birds for defects, "I think it mighta been one a' his girls."

"How come?"

"Who knows? Maybe she was jealous, maybe he didn't pay enough attention. You got to pay attention, you know—now don't go gettin' attitude when I say this, Mali, 'cause I know how you are—but it's like a farmer and his crop. You got to plant it properly, fertilize it, cultivate it and watch for weeds, water it before you can get a decent harvest."

I thought about it and I didn't get an attitude. It was a good analogy: cultivate and watch for weeds. Had Starr been a weed? Something to get rid of before her ideas infected the others?

And had he hooked her on drugs, not because Ozzie had beaten him, but because he needed to kill what he perceived to be her independence. Irony certainly had a place at this table. Short

Change had had no idea that her father also might have been afraid of her need for independence.

"My baby's dead," he had cried on the phone. But "baby" had courted death, it seemed, each time she had stepped away from him.

Had Ozzie wanted her to remain dependent? Had Short Change wanted her dependent, if not on him, then on something just as powerful?

"Do you think Short Change killed Starr?"

I watched him shrug and lift the lid from one of the pots again. He gave it a quick stir and adjusted the jet. I breathed in the heady aroma and determined to take home a large order when I left, even though I was not hungry. Yet.

"I just don't know, Mali. He was peculiar, as players go. Most pimps beat their women, scar 'em up so they ain't no good for nobody else, then send 'em on their way. But S.C.? I don't know about him. I think he got his kicks, got off just seein' her strung out, beggin' for a fix, promisin' to do anything to get it. People lose everything, you know, when they after that next hit. Especially they lose their self-respect. When that's gone, they open to anything. Anything. I think that's how Short Change got even. Let the world know she wasn't so tough-minded after all."

I stared out the restaurant's window onto the busy, sun-blasted sidewalk of Lenox Avenue and thought of Short Change and how Starr had told him to kiss her royal black ass. Had she really said this or was it all part of the loud and loose talk at the wake? Had she told him this in front of the crowd at the Casablanca? Even so, he probably hadn't killed her. The slow, humiliating process of addiction was much more rewarding than dispatching her with a swift, deep flick of a knife.

I left Charleston's place empty-handed because my order wouldn't be ready for another hour. I wasn't really hungry after plowing through that stack of waffles at Wells but this aroma had gotten to me.

"Jo Jo'll deliver it to your dad," he said, now pulling meaty slabs of ribs from the freezer.

I stepped out into the midday heat and walked over to the small triangle of park near St. Marks Church, where Edgecombe and St. Nicholas avenues converged in front of the old Harriet Beecher Stowe Junior High School. The school, once all girls, was now coed and renamed for Thurgood Marshall. The triangle was tree-shaded and quiet enough for me to relax and scribble the latest information in my notebook.

If Short Change hadn't killed Starr, who had?

My thoughts went back to Travis. Why hadn't he been on the cruise? What was he doing while his wife was making a spectacular nuisance of herself? Had something happened to make him turn on Starr and then go after Short Change?

Or perhaps, as Charleston said, it might have been two separate incidents. Short Change, after all, had been dabbling in the drug trade. Perhaps another dealer decided to eliminate the competition. And Ozzie. He was angry enough to wipe out an army. Why had he disappeared when he did? And now wanted to be left alone.

I put a check mark next to some of the questions, then closed the book. For a few minutes I remained on the bench, listening to the scattered songs of birds nesting in the branches overhead. An ICEY man passed, rolling his small cart. He turned the corner at 136th Street, heading toward Eighth Avenue. A minute later, I left the bench and headed for 135th Street.

The flower vendors in front of the hospital offered a wide choice and I selected a mix of roses, black-eyed Susans, and gladiolas. Although I was still on vacation, I stopped by my department, conferred with my supervisor, then took the elevator to the twelfth floor, where I donned a mask and gown and entered a room equipped with ultraviolet lighting and special ventilation.

Saturday—Sara Lee Brown—was propped up in bed reading. She closed the book as I approached.

"Well, I don't know who you are behind all that space suit, but if you bringin' flowers, you ain't a doctor. The doctors only come with needles, tubes, and more needles."

"It's me, Mali," I said, taking a seat near the bed. The ultraviolet light cast a surreal glow over the room and the quiet rush of air eliminated the usual antiseptic sick-room smell.

Sara Lee bent forward, saw my eyes, then smiled and leaned back against the pillows again. Although she had been here less than a week, the change in her appearance was dramatic. Her face looked less drawn; her eyes had lost the wandering stare and her hands seemed less bony and less shaky when she pressed the button for the nurse.

An aide opened the door, her eyes wide above the mask. "Yes, honey?"

"Sorry to disturb you," Sara Lee whispered. "I was wonderin' if I could get a vase or a jar or somethin' for these flowers. Ain't they nice?"

"Beautiful. I'll see what I can do."

The door closed again, leaving us in silence.

"So how're you doing?" I asked, knowing she'd probably had no visitors other than Jo Jo.

"Miss Mali, I can't thank you enough. You and Jo Jo saved my life. If it wasn't for you—"

She broke off and gazed at the flowers and started to cry. "You know how long it's been since anybody brought me flowers?"

I nodded, knowing what she really meant was "You know how long it's been since I felt this clean, this well, this hopeful?"

She fingered the petals on a rose as if the flower were an entirely new species and she would have examined it in more detail had she had access to a microscope. "Jo Jo been here every day since I came in," she said. Her voice was no longer a whisper and she gazed at me as if to say, "But I'm surprised to see you. Really surprised."

So I came right to the point.

"Sara, how well did you know Starr?"

She closed her eyes, still fingering the petals of the rose, and did not answer.

I decided to take another tack. "How well did you know Short Change?"

"Too well and not well enough," she murmured, turning to look at me.

"What do you mean?"

She set the bunch of flowers aside and I waited, listening to the soft rush of air wash the room in a rhythm of sound.

"You know," she said softly, "things happen, but mostly, the thing that you want, that you wish for, don't happen. And you live in hope, all of us. At least that's what we did. Amanda, Martha, Jeanette, Myrtle, and me."

"What about Starr?"

Sara Lee shook her head. "Unh-unh. Not Starr. She was the only one had some sense. But the rest of us, we lived waitin' for that something that never came."

A half smile crossed her face before she continued. "You know, S.C. liked to say, 'I'm gonna make you . . . get you . . . do this for you . . . do that . . . put your pretty self on stage . . . on the moon. On top of the world.' All that. Everything was a promise and we lived for it. Worked hard, 'cause we thought if we worked hard, he'd make it all come true. Well . . ."

She brushed her hands through her hair, tight-curled short hair with a growth of dark brown edging out the dull blond strands.

"We all knew the deal. We all knew but nobody spoke on it. Short Change was short on promise and everything else. Especially that main thing. That thing we were all lookin' for, beyond his word, his promise. It never happened. I don't know about the others 'cause it was never talked about, but I felt he had cheated me. Talked the talk and didn't have much to back it up with, except more talk."

She hesitated, unsure whether she wanted to continue. I waited while she drew a deep breath, then she went on.

"You know what got me evicted? One night I had just enough of that hundred-dollar champagne in me to let him know that I was tired. Tired of hearin' about how he got a stroke that ain't no joke. How once he get started, his shit don't quit. Well, where was it? I was bringin' in the money. Top dollar. That's why he chose me to live with him. So he could throw all them dollars up in the air and laugh when they come floatin' down. Where was his action at? And he come off with that Dr. Laura talk-show bullshit. Tryin' to play me, tellin' me some psychology shit about how sex is mostly in the mind. It ain't about so much action.

"Really? What he think I was? One a' them dumb cryin' and confused bitches on Jenny Jones? 'Cause that wasn't the first time he pulled that kinda talk. You know, I was out there turnin' a trick a minute. That's how good I was but it was work. I needed somethin' real when I got home and it just was not happenin'. So that night, I looked at him like I seen him for the first time and I said, 'Damn! So that's why she call you Short Change.' "

"Who called him that?"

"Starr did. Who you think?

"Now, I'm sayin' it's one thing to peep a player's hole card but it's another thing to speak on it. He wanted to know who she was. Wanted to know what was goin' on behind his back. But I wasn't talkin'. Next thing I knew, I found myself on the curb. No clothes, no nuthin' but what I had on my back, which wasn't much.

"For a while, I hustled on my own, stayed here, there, anywhere, tryin' to get myself together. Trickin' fast and hard and careless. And you know a lot of men pay extra not to use a condom. I didn't care one way or the other. It was like I was no good. No good. I got infected and didn't care. Kept goin' until I got too sick to even crawl half a block. And you know somethin'? Right now, sometimes, I wake up at night and listen in the dark. I hear him, still promisin', and I close my eyes and fall into a dream, and imagine that I could help him make the promise come true.

"Yes, Starr had called him Short Change and the name caught and spread like a fire out of control. She had called him that straight out. Told him he wasn't gonna be a part of her life and he could kiss her royal black ass."

"Did he kill her?"

She was silent for a moment and when she answered, she did not look at me.

"I don't know. Coulda been any one of the girls. They was all jealous of her, you know."

Which meant that she had been jealous also, despite that champagne and all those dollars floating in the air.

The door opened and the aide stepped in carrying a vase. She lifted the flowers from the bed and began to arrange them for maximum effect on the nightstand. Under the light, the colors seemed to expand before the stark gray of the walls and she stepped back to gauge her handiwork. "They look beautiful, don't you think?"

"Very much," I said, trying to match her cheerfulness. Sara Lee nodded but said nothing. Once I stepped out and the door closed, she would be alone.

"I'll bring some books when I come back," I said.

"Thank you, thanks for coming." She said this as if she expected not to see me again but to add me to the long list, another broken promise.

I went looking for the physician in charge, showed him

my unit ID and he allowed me to look at her chart. The protocol was pretty rigorous. INH, rifampin, pyrazinamide daily for two months, then INH twice a week for a total of nine months. In addition, there was a course of AZT and protease inhibitors for the HIV.

"She's a strong woman," he said. "She's young and wants to get well. I would say that the prognosis is good."

23

I reached home and Dad and I approached the door at the same time, I with my key in hand ready to step in, and he with Ruffin ready to step out.

"Glad you're here. Ozzie called."

"What happened?"

"He didn't say. Just said I should come down there right away."

His face was a map of anxiety and I quickly fell in step beside him, wondering how the hell all this was going to end. It was a few blocks before he spoke again. "I don't know what's up.

Maybe he wants to talk. Maybe being alone is finally getting to him, or maybe he found out something."

We hurried along 125th Street and turned south on Manhattan Avenue, passing Perk's Restaurant, where its satiny lights spilled through the curtains, illuminating the double- and triple-parked cars.

I caught soft sounds of laughter and thought of Tad, and a pain, deep and sudden, rose in my chest.

Ozzie did not answer the door. After the third ring Dad pulled out the key he had been given. "I had this all along but he said he needed to be alone. As upset as I was, there's some lines you can't cross. I had to respect that. I had to wait."

We stepped inside. The house seemed cavernous as we made our way through the darkened foyer. Our footsteps resonated on the hardwood floor and I heard nothing else except the tap of Ruffin's paws and the fast beat of my own heart.

A small lamp in the living room cast an ineffectual glow over the sofa and the two large chairs facing it. The rest of the room was in shadow. Ruffin halted suddenly and let out a low growl, then leaped forward, nearly pulling me off my feet. At the same time Ozzie, who was lying on the sofa, sat up with a start.

"What the hell—?"

"Take it easy, Ozzie," Dad whispered, stepping in front of Ruffin and grabbing the dog's collar. "Okay, Ruffin. Okay. It's all right."

Then he turned to Ozzie. "I'm sorry about that. I—"

Ozzie was sitting up now and waved his hand. "It's cool, man. Everything's cool. I must have nodded off."

He did not look well. He leaned over and shook his head as if to clear it, then rose to his feet but a second later sank heavily back onto the sofa again. I did not see a bottle or glass but the odor of alcohol hung in the air.

Dad took the leash from me and led Ruffin back to the foyer. I listened to the pad of paws, then the sound of him settling on the floor near the door.

"And don't move," Dad whispered.

Ozzie was now sprawled on the sofa, his arm across his face as if he were alone in the room. When Dad returned, he leaned over and touched Ozzie's shoulder. "What happened, man? You heard anything? What's going on?"

Ozzie did not answer, but pointed to a small frayed notebook that lay open on the coffee table.

"Read it," he whispered.

"What is it?"

"Her journal. Diary. Notes. Whatever you want to call it." I watched Dad hesitate, then he picked it up and held it gingerly in his hands. "Where did you find this?"

"Had it all along. Since the night she died. Took it before the cops got their hands on it. Go on. Read it. You too, Mali. Maybe there's something I missed. Something you might find to help explain why she did what she did."

He lay still again and I moved next to Dad and peered over his shoulder in the dim light.

Some of the entries were in ink, others were in pencil, and some of the pencil entries appeared faded or perhaps smudged. Some paragraphs were printed and others were written in a spidery, barely legible scrawl. There were no dates:

> Vegas nearly turned me inside out. It was like a dream I wanted to live inside of. Even when Henry suggested a

threesome which I wasn't about to get into. And not that other stuff either. He smiled when I said no and I misunderstood. That smile. Too late to say I was a fool. He saw me coming. Read the map of my face and knew which road I needed to take. He would be my guide.

What am I doing? What am I seeing? The awful way he dresses should have told me something. He wants the world to take notice. Or maybe he's color blind. But then I'm really the blind one. I thought I saw something beyond the way he dressed. It was the thing he said and the way he said it. Promising me. Fly me to the moon if only I wouldn't leave him. Travis says the same but not like that. Not with his mouth pressed against my stomach the way Henry does it. Henry talks fast and pays serious lip service between his words. Travis never made me feel like that no matter how he tried. Even when I want to show him. He is too wound up. Chrissie is kicking his ass.

I'm free. At least for a while. Dad took care of him. Travis would have done it. Wanted to shoot him but Dad got to him first with that pipe.

I should sing, Travis says. Well dammit I know that. I know that. What I need is for him to tell me he loves me. I need to hear it. Then maybe my head would be straightened out and I'd walk away from this stuff once and for all.

Dad, I'm sorry. What a disappointment I am. I can see it in your face every time you look at me, look at my legs and look away. I see your rage and I know some of it's aimed at me. And it should be. How could I have done this? Now it seems so stupid, so destructive. Maybe I wanted you or maybe Travis to pull me out of the next thing I'd managed to get myself into.

Henry was feeding me so much Black Tar shit I thought I was an honorary Mexican. I'm killing Dad because I'm killing myself. Must find a way to stop this. One time I got so tired I took a "hot shot." To sleep forever. Sail into the hereafter as high as I could get. It's first thing in the morning when I wake. I need a fix. Then I go back to sleep and dream of how I'm going to get the next one. He feeds me "one on ones," a quarter of H and a dime of coke. Forget food. Forget family. Heroin feeds whatever hunger you have. Forget everything but being hungry for the next hit. It's like being in heaven and hell.

What day is this. Gotten so bad I am completely in love with heroin, would marry it if I could . . .

Dad. I'm sorry. I felt ground giving way with each step. The further the walk, the greater the distance, the softer the sand sucking around my ankles. I felt it, knew it, and wouldn't turn back. You pulled me out of the swamp but now my legs, my legs look as if rats had gotten to them.

Pain. I would do anything to make it stop. I shot three grams and I didn't die. I didn't die and I'm pissed off. I didn't die, dammit.

I don't know why or how I let him talk me into this. He did it because he hated you, Dad. I mean you love me. That's why you beat him and nearly killed him. Nobody had ever loved him like you loved me and he couldn't understand.

I know now that I need to breathe. I'm clean now and have everything but the air I need in order to live. I am smothered. Twenty-eight and still the little girl whom you don't want to see grow up. Maybe if Mom had been here, it would've been different. I'm making excuses again. I purposely went looking for a way out. Tried to test myself by hanging on the edge and, still being the little girl, I figured if I let go I'd fly rather than fall. And if I fell, you or somebody would be there. I look at my veins now and I can't find them. They're all used up.

Glad I told him to kiss my ass. Since that's all he seemed able to do. I was tired of lip service. He short-changed me and everybody else, only everybody else doesn't know it. I can't believe I was so stupid.

I testified and glad I did. Didn't know much about [smudged] operation but knew he kept a lot in the spare, the glove compartment and in that custom made slot [smudged] below the cup holder.

Travis called. Spoke for two hours. Finally made up his mind to leave her, not for me, I think. But for his sanity. Which is well. I don't need a crazy person to love. I'm crazy enough.

Travis is coming here. I'm telling him that it's all over. And my business will be settled.

Ozzie was sitting up again when Dad closed the book.

"What do you think?"

"I don't know, Ozzie. It's hard to say anything behind this. No parent wants to see his kid fail, but sometimes—"

Ozzie quieted him with a wave of his hand. "What did she

mean by needing to breathe? That she was bein' smothered? What did she mean?"

Before Dad could frame an answer, he went on. "You know, Jeffrey, I tried my best. The best I could. Took every gig that came my way, through good times and bad. Worked them all 'cause I never knew when bad times would come around again. Everything comes in cycles, you know. Everything. So I made hay. And we tried to give her all the stuff I never had, you know, private school, music, the tennis. I didn't realize . . ."

He closed his eyes and raised both hands, palms up, as if to extract the answer from the air. Then just as quickly he dropped them and gripped his knees. "I shoulda called you earlier, Jeffrey, but I needed time to try to figure this out. That's all I've been doin', night and day and night. I sit by that window and watch dawn break, thinkin' this is the day the answer's gonna come to me. Then at night, I dream and try to piece together something from the dream. A sign or something. I come up with nothing. Nothing."

What about Travis? I wanted to ask. That was the last entry in the journal. There was not a line after that, but I decided to keep quiet until I could speak to Travis myself.

I looked from Ozzie to my father and back again and wondered in the silence that surrounded us if, this time, Starr's wake had finally begun.

At 3 A.M. I took Ruffin and walked home. On the way I stopped by Charleston's to order some food for Dad and Ozzie but Jo Jo had gone home hours ago.

"Things is slow around this time so I'm a lock up in a minute and make the run myself," Charleston said as he filled two large take-out orders.

"You'd do that for me?"

"Hell no, not for you. But for the piano man. I like his sounds and want to keep on hearing them."

He winked and I laughed. A minute later I

stepped out onto Malcolm X Boulevard. There had been no break in the heat and the avenue was crowded with folks strolling as casually as if they were making a run to the neighborhood bodega at high noon. Cars moved with stereos blasting in their wake; tenement stoops were crowded and those who were able to sleep in the apartments above did so with windows opened wide to the noise of the night. Whirring fans rotated below knotted curtains, trying in vain to pull in a wisp of air.

A few people detoured at the sight of Ruffin and one commented on his size: "What do you feed your horse, sister?" This from a stoop lounger poised to fly inside his apartment if Ruffin so much as yawned.

I chose not to answer but waved and continued walking, zigzagging through the blocks to Powell Boulevard. I passed under the weathered marquee of the old Renaissance Ballroom and hurried across the avenue just as the light changed.

A step ahead of me, a man with a distinctive, pigeon-toed walk turned at the sound of Ruffin and froze at the sight of him.

"My God, that's a big dog . . ."

"Yes, he is," I said. "I hope we didn't frighten you."

I looked at Travis Morgan as he stared at Ruffin. "Is he a show dog?" he asked, keeping a careful distance.

"Not exactly," I said, "but he's worth his weight in gold, diamonds, and platinum."

"Now that's what I call love," he said.

When he laughed, he tilted his head and half closed his eyes. He has nice teeth, I thought. His teeth are bright and perfect just like Tad's.

"I'm Mali Anderson," I said and waited in the silence for him to make the connection. He gazed at me for a second and then extended his hand. "Right. Mali Anderson, the bass player's daughter. I've seen you at the club. You know Ozzie Hendrix."

"I also knew his daughter," I said. "As a child, Starr came to my house several times with her dad. For rehearsals."

I watched Travis's shoulders fall and a fire seemed to go out of his eyes as he glanced away. "Small world, isn't it," he murmured. "How's her father, how's he holding—?"

"Not too well," I whispered. "As a matter of fact, I'm trying to help him find out what he can about her death."

I heard the deep intake of breath and caught his sidelong glance as we turned into Strivers Row.

There is never a good time or place to talk about death. We were not in a bar, where that second drink might help to recall a forgotten detail, or, if necessary, quench painful memory; we were not in a restaurant, or even sitting in a park.

A walk would have to do, so I did not stop, but moved on past my house. We walked past the other houses with their closed windows and drawn curtains, and small ornamental lights casting warm pools of yellow on the front steps.

At intervals, the streetlights pulled our shadows before us and I remembered the childhood game of skipping and jumping and trying to catch up, and the shadow always remaining a step ahead.

"I saw Starr the day she was killed," Travis whispered. "The same day. We had some words and—"

"Words? What did you argue about?"

"Well, it wasn't exactly an argument. I had phoned her and she said she had to see me, wanted to tell me something. I went over there but what she told me, I didn't want to hear. Wasn't prepared for it, I guess."

"What happened then?"

"I left. Said I was going someplace to cool off."

"Where'd you go?"

"No place in particular. Just walked. Just like I'm doing now. I was trying to make sense of what she'd said. How it would be better if we didn't see each other anymore. She had to get her life on track. 'Move on' was the way she put it. And I just wasn't prepared to hear that."

His voice had dropped to a whisper and he strode with his head down as if the cracked pavement would reveal the answer to his confusion.

"You know, this'll sound strange but she had become like an anchor. Even when she was going through her bad time, I always felt I needed her more than she needed me. I loved her. I never imagined we'd be apart."

"Not ever?"

He stopped and shook his head. "I know what you're asking," he said, gazing at me. "Here I am a married man trying to eat his cake and have it too. Trying to play the game, both ends against the middle. That's what you're thinking, right? Well, even if I sound like I'm lying, I want you to know that I was working on a divorce when Starr died. That's the truth. Starr was special. She was talented and passionate about what she wanted out of life."

"What did she want?"

He stopped again to stare at me. "You're asking me what she wanted and you knew her all her life?"

"I knew she had at one time wanted to be the best damn jazz singer there ever was," I replied. "She wanted to be like Sarah, Ella, and Betty Carter."

"Ah . . . yes." He grew silent as we reached Frederick Douglass Boulevard and turned south, moving under the shade trees gracing the front of the St. Charles townhouses. We walked past the Harlem Collective boutique and at 135th Street strolled back to Powell Boulevard. He spoke again when we paused in front of the sealed windows of the old Small's Paradise.

"Starr had plans," he said, gazing at the traffic moving past us. "She was very direct. Said no one was going to detour her again. To hell with everybody. When she said that, I knew it was only a matter of time before she said good-bye to me but even so, until that time I was willing to hang on to a small part of her. I just didn't think the time would come so soon.

"It's one thing for someone to say good-bye, maybe move to another town, even another country. There's always that chance you'll run into them again. But when the person dies, that good-bye is forever."

He gazed across the avenue, adrift in memory. I let a minute pass before I spoke.

"Who do you think killed her?"

It took several seconds for him to answer. The sweat glistened on his face and neck and on the brown triangle of chest where his silk shirt was unbuttoned. He had really nice features, thick eyebrows and a strong jawline. I remembered what Amanda said about his pigeon-toed walk. He was a good-looking brother and I wondered if Starr had been the only other woman in his life besides his wife.

"That pimp, that damn pimp killed her! Son of a bitch stopped everything. Stopped her life, everything."

He was shaking now and said this loud enough for a couple passing by to turn and stare. When they moved on, I said, "And did you kill him?"

"No, but I wish I had."

"It was your gun they found at the scene."

"I know it but I didn't do it."

"How could someone have gotten hold of your weapon?"

He shook his head now. "It's like I told Miss Jackson. The weapon was in the store. Under the counter near the register. The place is crowded most of the time, people asking questions, parents bringing the kids in for accessories. Folks just dropping in to talk about the latest software. As busy as the place is, I don't have an assistant yet."

"So anyone could've reached under there, picked it up, sold it for some quick cash, and it ends up being used in a murder," I said.

"Stolen guns are used in murders all the time," he said. "Except that my prints were found in her apartment. The police are saying I was out to avenge Starr's death."

We continued down Powell Boulevard, passing the Jamaican Hot Pot. I felt a strong hunger pang and wished the restaurant had been open. I could have hitched my horse to a parking meter and we could have stopped in for a fried shrimp dinner and a glass of sorrel.

"Do you usually stroll around at this late hour?" I asked. Of course he could have asked the same of me but he shrugged again.

"Only when I have to figure something out," he murmured. "Right now, I'm in the process of retrieving some data from my hard drives. Some of the units have been tampered with. The systems are down and I've hired someone to help me retrieve the information. Walking helps me to figure things out."

At 139th Street, we parted company and I turned into the block. I was alone with Ruffin and it was empty and quiet enough for me to pick up a sound of movement beyond the pad of his paws. His ears had perked up and he was alert. I turned quickly, only to stare at an empty street where light and shadow played through the thick-leaved trees. Had someone slipped between the parked cars? Or deep within the hedges of one of the gardens?

An icy awareness crept up my spine and I remembered the old folks saying: "When you shake like that means somebody walkin' on your grave."

I thought of the masked man and his parting words. My hand

went to my pocket and I palmed the small canister of mace as I unlocked the door.

Inside I called Dad to see if he was okay. What I really needed was to hear his voice, hear him cough, hiccup, sneeze, make some noise to connect me to anything but the specter I imagined hovering just beyond the locked door.

"Yeah, we're fine, Mali. The food arrived. Ozzie downed enough to take care of a busload of starvin' dudes. That Charleston can cook, I'm tellin' you."

I calmed down then, relaxed enough to fix a cup of chamomile tea, shower, and then climb into bed knowing that Ruffin was on duty at the front door. But sleep didn't come easily. All the ins and outs of Starr's diary—the things she had said and the stuff she didn't—played in my head. I thought of Ozzie struggling to understand and come to terms with her need for "air to breathe."

I wanted to know more about S.C.'s lip service and why Travis had not killed him. He certainly had been angry enough. And the final notation in Starr's diary was about Travis. He was coming to see her.

There was nothing after that.

The thing I liked about the Lenox Lounge was that you could step in at any time and find something happening, something going on: the jukebox blasting, a combo playing, the piano man in the back riffing through a new number, a middle-aged couple in the middle of the floor dancing with arms entwined and eyes closed as if they were in the center of their own living room.

There's the clatter of conversation. Laughter curling up through the smoke of cigarettes to graze against the leather ceiling. The door opening to admit a breath of new air and a new face to scan the old ones and New Face stepping out again to disappear into the flow of the crowded avenue.

When I stepped in, Too Hot was not there. I looked at my watch then slipped into the booth nearest the door, ordered an Absolut currant on the rocks with an orange juice chaser, and decided to wait. It was early evening and the place was just getting crowded. The piano man was into his sound, the door opened and closed, and folks came and went.

I sipped my drink and thought of Alvin, who would be home in less than a week. His call had awakened me and I could hear the crash of the surf in the background as he spoke. "Like I said, Mali. This is the bomb, but I gotta kick it with the crew for a few days before school starts. I gotta work out on the court and connect with Clarence before he leaves for Savannah State College."

Through the usual bad connection, he could barely contain his enthusiasm. "You know, Clarence is gonna be on the basketball team, and all them honeys are gonna be fallin' on him like rain."

Dad, who had been on the extension, cut in. "*Those* honeys, Alvin. And Clarence is going to hit those books or he'll hit the road and wind up back here with no degree and no future."

"Yeah, I know, Grandpa. That's why I have to hook up with my boy before he leaves. He's gonna be into some serious study down there."

"Just so you understand that, son."

"Oh, I understand. Yes, sir. I understand. That why I think I oughta come home before he leaves."

"We miss you too," I said. "We'll be glad to see you."

I thought about him and wondered how much taller he'd gotten since I'd last seen him six weeks ago. Some boys seemed to grow a foot a day.

My thoughts wandered and I remembered last night's encounter with Travis and decided that Chrissie was a fool. Then again, maybe so was I. The idea of calling Tad began to take shape and I thought of what I could say to apologize. Just then the door opened and Too Hot stepped in and moved toward the bar. He smiled at the barmaid, peeked into the back room to wave at the piano player, then turned and worked his way through the crowd again.

I held up my hand and he came over and sat beside me. As usual, he was impeccably dressed in a light gray linen suit, white shirt, and dark tie. He always wore a tie, perfectly knotted, even in toaster-hot temperatures. His cologne left a faint apple fragrance when he moved.

"Miss Mali. What's goin' on?"

He removed his hat and placed it on the table as the barmaid strolled over. She was tall, thin, and in good humor.

"What're you havin' today?"

"You forgot?"

"No, but sometimes folks like to change up every now and then," she said, glancing from me to give him a meaningful look. Too Hot caught the look and the message behind it. "This is Jeffrey Anderson's daughter," he said by way of introduction and advising by his formality that the meeting was strictly on the up-and-up. She looked at me again and straightened her shoulders. "I'm sorry. How are you?"

"Fine," I said.

"So bring me my usual," Too Hot said, "and another drink for Miss Anderson."

"Yes, sir."

She practically saluted before she left us.

"I don't mean to be so hard," he sighed, shaking his head as she moved across the floor, "but sometimes it don't pay to be too friendly."

I nodded, wondering how he could avoid it. He was a fixture

on the scene and everyone knew him and he knew everyone. Even though he had retired from his lucrative numbers business, he still held title to several parcels of private and commercial property in the area. So it was not friendship so much as respect that he expected.

An older barmaid would have known but this one was young, new on the scene, and didn't know his history. When she returned to the table, she placed the glasses on the table as if she were handling votive candles and quietly made her way back to the bar.

"She'll learn," he said, brightening up after the first sip and leaning back to survey the crowd. "So how's my man?"

"Dad's hanging in," I said.

"I mean my other man, Ozzie."

"About the same."

He continued to scan, smile, and nod his head slightly as folks circulated in, out, and back again to check if they had missed anything.

"So Ozzie's about the same?"

"Just barely—"

"Well, this might help." He leaned closer and his voice dropped to a feathery whisper against the beat of the jukebox, which by now had supplanted the piano man.

"Word on the street is that some woman was seen leavin' Starr's place. In a rush. Cut down those steps like somethin' was steppin' on her shadow."

I put my glass down. "A woman?"

"A tall one, about your height, and had real nice legs."

"What did she look like?"

"They didn't see the face. Only the legs. Short skirt and fancy shoes."

"How fancy?" I asked, thinking of any one of Short Change's women in their hootchie heels. I wondered how I could have been suckered in at that so-called wake but those women were good at gaming. Each was an actress if only for ten minutes at a time; longer if the price was right. If nothing else, that wake let me know that any one of them would have gladly changed places with Starr, stepped out of the life and into something, anything else, if they could. But they didn't and some had probably nursed a special bitterness.

One of them had probably been glad that Starr'd gotten strung out, and when she'd climbed back out of the sewer, the hatred flared again and she'd decided to kill Starr. It was easier than killing herself. Was that how it happened?

"This woman," I said, "was she young, old, in between, or what?"

Too Hot shrugged. "All I heard was that it was a woman in a hurry leavin' that building about the time Starr was killed. And that she was hikin' on some legs that was well put together."

"Okay. Okay," I said, trying to move him beyond the fixation on the legs. "Nobody saw her face, so what did the shoes look like?"

"Fancy."

"Fancy like what?" I persisted, thankful that I wasn't paying by the minute for him to let go of this information. It was like pulling a deep-rooted wisdom tooth.

"Were they fancy like high heels, open-toes, sling backs, lace ups, ankle straps, sandals, with bells jingling, lights flashing, what?"

"Bells," he said.

I looked at him in the dim light to see if he was laughing at me. He raised his glass to his mouth, took a sip, and placed it carefully on the table, where he rolled it back and forth in the curve of his fingers.

"High heels with bells," he said again.

Bells. I walked up Powell Boulevard thinking of circus clowns and belly dancers. And trying to figure out who in her right mind would wear shoes that announced her presence; shoes that sounded an alarm, that said, "*Ding, ding*, I'm here to kill you."

I thought of those firefly sneakers that lit up when pressure was placed on the heel and how those brilliant muggers were caught by their tracer lights as they fled the scene of the crime.

But those were sneakers, stupid design, yet the result was the same. Whoever legged it down those steps had not been thinking too clearly. High heels with bells.

I thought of the pile of shoes and boots that lay in the corner of Amanda's living room but Too Hot had said the woman was tall, about my height. Even with stilts, Amanda would probably have only reached to my shoulder, so it probably wasn't her.

I felt frustrated because I knew better than to ask Too Hot for his source. It had probably been the ICEY man making one of his night runs, and he did not want to be tagged. With no source, I couldn't go to the police. Not that I'd go in any event. It was understood that this information was for Ozzie and Ozzie alone, to do with as he saw fit.

I decided to tell him as much as I knew and let him take it from there. The prospect of having to visit Amanda and her crew again just to gauge their height, check their legs, and possibly peep at their shoes did not thrill me. But then again, with the state Ozzie was in, he'd demand to know my source; he'd speak to Too Hot, then probably track Sno and demand to know what else he might have seen.

And maybe the woman wasn't connected to Starr's death at all. Just someone leaving in a hurry to catch a cab.

Thursday dawned with rain threatening some relief from the broil-and-bake ambience. At eight o'clock, the thermostat outside the window was already pointing upward to 78 degrees and even the birds had taken a break.

By the time I showered and dressed, Dad had already walked Ruffin and was at the table with his second cup of coffee.

"I picked up some news yesterday at the Lenox Lounge," I

said, filling my cup. "Too Hot got the word that a woman was seen leaving Starr's place around the time she was killed."

Dad put his cup down and looked at me. "A woman? Did he say who she was? What she looked like?"

"He doesn't know. Only knows that she had good legs, real pretty legs, he said, and she wore fancy shoes. High heels with bells."

"You're kidding."

"Well, I asked him twice and that's what he said."

"Who's his source?"

"I think it's Sno."

"The ICEY man? Why?"

"Because he lives in that neighborhood. He's out at all hours and if he wasn't on the scene, he probably got the word from someone who was."

"I should've known. Guy sees everything, especially on his night shift. You gotta tell Ozzie."

I shrugged. "Not yet. I need some more information, something solid. Ozzie's feeling bad enough as it is. No point in sending him on a chase where he'll hit a brick wall."

In my room minutes later, the sound of Cyrus Chestnut's piano wizardry floated up as I pored over my notes. He had been aboard ship and Tad had purchased his CD for me as soon as we went ashore at Newport. I closed the book, lay back on the bed, and allowed the music to drift over me.

The trip seemed now like a magical moment that had happened a long time ago. Even the stopover at Nova Scotia, where we'd visited the black museum and spent so much time there we had to move fast to beat the deadline back to the ship.

I rolled over now to examine a map the curator had given me—a blueprint detailing the sea routes of blacks escaping from the unimaginable horror of slavery. In 1796, 543 Maroons sailed from Jamaica to Halifax, Nova Scotia. Then in 1800 they sailed to

Sierra Leone. Thirty-five hundred loyal blacks left New York City in 1783 for Halifax (probably after the British defeat) and from there, 1,190 sailed to Sierra Leone in 1792. Between 1813 and 1815, 1,200 black refugees sailed from the Chesapeake Bay and Delaware Bay areas, and 2,500 more sailed from Jamaica to settle in Dartmouth, Nova Scotia.

I regretted not having had more time to study this chapter of black history so new to me. But Tad and I and several others had had to rush to catch a bus, a fast-moving ferry, another bus, and managed to step aboard the ship's tender three minutes before the whistle blew.

In the cabin, we spent a half hour catching our breath as the ship cleared the harbor and headed for Newport.

"You hungry?" he asked.

"For dinner?"

"Yeah."

"Not right now," I murmured, stretching out on the bed. I closed my eyes and relaxed under the warm touch of his fingers on my legs.

The whistle sounded and the ship pushed lightly on a calm sea. We settled onto the thick carpet near the bed and lost track of time. Later, I pushed the curtains aside and a narrow shaft of moonlight fell across Tad's stomach like a pale ribbon. I traced the ribbon with my bottom lip. I heard him murmur something. I felt the quick draw of his breath and the rise of his stomach against my face and lost track of time again.

I clicked off the music, grabbed my bag, and quickly left the house. I needed to leave that kind of memory behind.

Out in the street, I was able to breathe easier. On Powell Boulevard, it seemed as if everyone had left town. Even the ball court behind the "Y" was empty as I cut over to Malcolm X Boulevard. A few hardy vendors sat broiling under their umbrellas outside Pan Pan's restaurant and sunglasses seemed to be the big sale item.

At 132nd Street the Club Harlem's elegant canopy stretched to the curb and the lush planters flanked the double-height teak door like sentries. A couple strolled by pushing a baby carriage. An old man with a cane carved with African warrior faces walked his dog. A boy on a bike rolled by wearing a T-shirt that read: THE STREET CRIME UNIT WELCOMES YOU TO NEW YORK. NOW DUCK!

I paused in the sliver of shade the canopy offered and wondered if any of them were aware of the tragedy that hung over the club's piano man. Ozzie's picture was still posted among that of the other musicians but no one, not even Dad, knew when he'd return. I knew it wouldn't be any time soon.

Short Change, as it turned out, did not own a brownstone facing Marcus Garvey Park as rumor had it. Even the news articles that reported his death had it all wrong. He had actually been shot near the park and, in the best tabloid tradition, his living space had been confused with his final resting place.

I doubled back to Charleston, got the right address from his delivery book, and twenty minutes later found myself standing in front of a narrow, three-story limestone on 121st Street between

Powell Boulevard and Malcolm X Boulevard where Short Change had once rented the parlor floor and basement.

A few doors away from the house, a woman tending a Green Thumb community garden greeted me. I pointed to the tree near the fence, surprised to see one in Harlem growing real peaches.

"Well, look some more," she said, nodding toward the three apple trees, a fig tree, a cherry tree, and two additional peach trees, one of which she said she'd planted three years ago.

"Ain't nuthin' to it," she said, "if you got the right spirit. I simply ate the peach, enjoyed it, and stuck the little pit down in the soil. We also got lettuce, radishes, squash, collards, mustard greens, pole beans, cucumbers, and the tomatoes are so big you got to roll 'em away. Too heavy to carry."

She lay the water hose aside and opened the chain-link fence, allowing me to enter. The small footpath led to a seat under the largest apple tree, which rose up about ten or twelve feet. The garden was narrow, situated as it was between two houses, but it was deep, running back about ninety feet.

This spot of Eden was so beautiful I wondered when our mayor, the Rude One, would get the word and send in his boys to bulldoze it as he had done with the other community gardens. Thank God for Bette Midler stepping to the plate in time to save at least some of them.

The spot under the tree was shady and the bench, fashioned from slats of cedar set on two pieces of recycled concrete, was quite comfortable. I watched the lady snake the hose up and down the rows, soaking the plants as she spoke.

"Yep, I know the boy you askin' about. If you know ten folks in Harlem, you know 'em all and everybody knows you."

I introduced myself and mentioned my dad. She stepped back when she heard his name and clapped her hand to her mouth. "Well, I'll be . . . I know your daddy, the bass player. Used to run into him years ago in one a' them after-hour spots. Now that was a jumpin' joint. I went there every Friday and shook a leg 'til the sun come up. Had on my yellow dress and high heels and my hair was fried, dyed, and laid to the side.

"Ain't been to that new club yet. Prices too rich and my social security don't stretch but so far. But I'm glad he doin' good. You tell 'im Miss Babe said hello. Yep, I used to be real skinny back then and that yellow dress was sayin' a lot. Girl needed something special to stand out in all that crowd. Anyway, I don't know if he'll remember me but he oughta remember that dress. Everybody does."

She shaded her eyes against the sun and smiled at her handiwork.

"See? Not a weed in sight. Anyway, the boy you talkin' about, his name was Henry Stovall but somewhere along the way, he picked up the name Short Change."

"How'd he get that name? Did he cheat anybody out of something?"

"Well," she adjusted her wide-brimmed straw hat and eased down on the bench beside me. Her dark face was smooth and seamless and her skin held a cinnamon scent. She had hands that were large and strong-looking and they lay loosely in her lap as she spoke.

"I'd say it was more like somebody cheated him. You know that boy grew up around here. Born on Lenox, three doors away from Mickey Funeral, the Carolina Service. Then his mama moved here into the block with him. She was one of them party girls but kinda calmed down after he came. She got a regular job, sent him to school, kept his clothes neat. Everything.

"But you know how some kids get when Mama can't come up with a' answer that makes sense when they ask about Daddy? See, that's the trouble with the race. The men are made invisible.

They're made invisible and it ain't their fault. It goes back too far to remember when it was different. And we still fightin' against them odds. Gone men, grievin' women, sufferin' children. You know, just like in a war.

"Well, in addition to that, this child really got a bad deal. Cheated, is what I call it. When he was real young, one of his testicles didn't drop the way it was supposed to as he was developin' and later it turned to cancer. His mama panicked and instead a' goin' to Harlem Hospital, where the folks really give a damn about you, she took 'im someplace downtown and he come back with his equipment useless. Now I got this straight from the vine so I know what I'm talkin' about. He had some other kinda treatment but it didn't do no good."

"You mean he couldn't have any children?" I said, putting it as delicately as I could.

"He couldn't do a thing." Miss Babe sighed. "And you know, somethin' like that is enough to kill a man. But Henry was strange. He made up his mind to make good out of bad. He went into somethin', the same life his mama had fought so hard to move away from. When he started gatherin' up all those women and young girls, his mama said he was doin' it to prove somethin' to himself; that he could outfish any fisherman. In other words, pull in a sizable catch without usin' real bait."

"What did he use?" I asked.

Miss Babe glanced at me and in the short silence adjusted the straw brim so that only her nose and mouth showed.

"Ah, well. You know how we folks make do. Make a way out of no way. Plus he had a gift for gab. A real gift. Boy shoulda been a preacher. Woulda made the same money and with less complications. Now look. He went and killed that girl and somebody turned around and killed him. Folks don't believe how what goes around comes around, but that's what happened to him."

She rose from the bench, moved to the rear of the garden, and returned with three tomatoes the size of melons.

"Sorry I don't have a bag to put 'em in, but they're nice and ripe so don't drop 'em."

With that she picked up the hose again and I thanked her and left. I walked quickly, balancing the tomatoes in the crook of my arm, and trying to balance the image of Henry Stovall, an impotent pimp who had only lip service to offer, who somehow managed to shortchange everyone.

27

Back home, at my desk, I picked up my pen but didn't know where or how to begin. Henry Stovall: The man had been able to sweep women into his orbit despite a serious handicap. Then along came Starr to tell him she was tired of lip service, to kiss her ass.

The other women had probably been too mesmerized, too needy, frightened, or hopeless but Starr—and to some extent, Sara Lee—had laid it on the line. One had been thrown out, the other was killed.

I closed the book but opened it again just as

quickly. Who was the girl with the fancy shoes? Had S.C. sent someone to do the job? I thought of the women at the wake whose loud personal testimonies had hidden so much other stuff; I couldn't decide which of them might have done it. Amanda had been the only one to seriously praise Starr and it turned out that she'd been the most jealous.

I was going in circles so I closed the book, and prepared a bubble bath steeped with lavender salts. That usually cleared my head.

When I stepped out of the tub, the clock said 4 P.M. I gathered the notebook, which lay near Tad's packet, and toyed with the idea of mailing the pictures to him with a sweet note. Then a fresh wave of anger hit as I opened the package again.

I sifted through the pictures, feeling like a religious flagellant scourging myself to atone for past and present sins and to lay up heavenly credits for future bad stuff.

The more I stared at the pictures, the more I hurt. The more I hurt, the more intensely I itched to roll up on Chrissie again and rearrange the smug, ugly face that smiled back at me.

One picture caught my eye and I was studying it closely when the phone rang.

Elizabeth's voice filtered through from the lobby of the state Supreme Court, her cell phone picking up all the background pandemonium.

"What?" I yelled.

"You don't have to yell," she shouted through the crackling. "I can hear you perfectly."

"What did you say?"

"Travis has been indicted for Henry Stovall's murder."

"Oh, shit!"

"What?"

"Nothing," I said, wishing the connection were clearer.

"Look, Mali, I want you to meet me at the office in an hour."

When I arrived, Elizabeth was pacing the floor. Travis's file lay open on her desk and behind her thoughtful expression, I knew she was worried.

"I hadn't expected an indictment," she said. "I thought we had compelling evidence that he was not the one. Somehow the assistant district attorney zeroed in on the whereabouts of the gun the night of the murder, questioned him about his impending divorce, and portrayed him as someone jealous and dangerous."

"Was his bail revoked?"

"No. I managed to reach a judge, a sister, who believes that an indictment is just that. An indictment, not a finding of guilt. So he's still out."

"What do you want me to do?"

"I'm not sure. He said he'd spoken to you the other night. Tell me again what he said. I need to see if there are any holes in his story, any contradictions."

"Is that his file?"

"Yes."

"Can I scan it without breaking any laws or rules of confidentiality?"

"Technically, as of one minute ago, you're now on the case. Working for me, so to speak. We'll worry about licensing later."

"Okay," I said, reaching for the file. "When I send you my bill, don't faint, but here's what I have so far."

I went over Travis's conversation again, filled her in on the contents of Starr's journal, Henry Stovall's special history, and the girl with the fast-and-fancy shoes who may or may not have been rushing out for a taxi.

Elizabeth sat at her desk, jotting the new information on a legal pad. I moved to the small table near the window to examine his file. It had been divided into two parts. "Civil," dealing with the divorce action, and "Criminal," dealing with Henry Stovall's murder. I was looking for the small things, the mundane items that might provide answers to some of the larger questions.

I leafed through a dozen pages in the civil material before coming to a five-by-eight brown envelope. The contents spilled out when I lifted it and I studied receipts, charge copies, and old, canceled checks.

"Travis hasn't canceled his charge cards or checking account yet? What's he waiting for?"

Elizabeth, who was going over her own notes, stopped to examine some of the checks. "I advised him to do this a while ago but seems he never got around to it. I suppose he was too distracted to take care of business as he should have."

"Travis doesn't open his own mail?" I asked.

"Not if he recognizes it as a bill. He knows who it's from and it stresses him out so he sends them on to me. I'll add them up and eventually he'll deal with the one grand total."

"Starr must have meant a lot to him," I said.

"She did."

"But he didn't kill Henry Stovall," I said.

"I don't believe so either but thinking he's innocent and

knowing he's innocent are two different things. We've got to find enough evidence to create a reasonable doubt."

She sat at her desk again and studied her notes. I continued to work but slower now, carefully examining each receipt one by one and setting a few aside as I moved along.

"And those aren't all," Elizabeth said. "I expect at least a few more to trickle in before all this is over. I mean wifey is a damn big spender. The guy is totally stressed out."

I looked at more receipts, tucked some of the charge slips in another envelope, and placed the envelope in my bag.

"I'll return these as soon as possible," I said, closing the file.

"What's your next move?"

"I don't know yet," I said. "I'll have to think about this as I go along."

I hurried home, changed my outfit, and then took the subway downtown. At 70th Street, I walked over to Madison Avenue, the heart of boutique country. The store I was looking for was decorated in up-to-the-minute, spare, minimalist style and a small bell chimed discreetly when I stepped in.

I was wearing my favorite outfit from Gourd Chips—a diagonally cut white linen sheath, and a necklace of large dark amber. My straw brim, black patents, and Hollywood sunglasses completed the picture.

One of three saleswomen quickly sized me up, calculated the probable heft of my charge plate, and put on a wide smile as she approached.

"Good evening, madam."

She was well trained and did not squint as if I were a stick-up artist casing the place.

Instead, she seemed to purr. "My name is Dori. Look around and let me know if I may be of assistance."

"Well, yes, I think you can," I smiled, pulling out a photo from my bag. "I'm interested in a pair of shoes like these. My girlfriend, who was aboard the *QE2* with me, said she bought them here."

The saleswoman looked at the picture, heard *"QE2,"* and smelled more dollars. She smiled wider.

"Of course. Of course. We remember her very well."

That was the cue for the other saleswomen to crowd around and gaze at the picture and murmur appropriate "ahhs" as I described the jazz cruise and the compliments Chrissie's shoes received.

"Very, very special customer," Dori went on as if recalling the late Princess Di. "These shoes were custom-made. We had something close to it in stock but she didn't want them. She wanted something unique so we designed a pair. We do that, you know, for our special customers."

She turned to the other saleswomen, who by now had crowded even closer to admire the photo of Chrissie leaning against the stateroom door, one hand on her hip, the other above her head to add distance between her rib cage and waist. The shoes, ringed with tiny bell-like objects, accentuated her foxy legs and she smiled and smiled.

I smiled also and shook my head. "How much would a pair—not exactly like this, but something slightly different—cost? I mean, I don't want to cause complications by copying her style, you know what I mean?"

"Of course. Of course. No one likes to see themselves coming and going. No one. Especially a person of your good taste. Actually, your friend has the only pair like it. We wouldn't dream of copying it. So we appreciate that you'd like something a little different."

The other saleswomen nodded in unison and murmured a chorus of "nooo," like Madonna's backup singers.

Without losing her smile and calculating faster than I could blink, Dori said, "Six hundred and fifty dollars and three weeks delivery."

I thought I heard my throat constrict. I tried not to blink too hard and my face was beginning to ache from smiling so tightly. Finally, I said, "My fiancé gave me a birthday gift to spend any way I wished. May I have your card? I want to think about this and decide on a color. When I come again, I'll bring him with me."

Outside, I walked quickly in the humid evening air, not quite recovered from the price quote. The avenue was crowded with the end-of-the-day rush of people heading homeward. Some of the shops were closing but the windows of most of them remained as bright and inviting as a Christmas scene. I ignored everything, thinking of this new development.

This changes everything, I thought. Complicates things. It wasn't Chrissie running down those stairs. She had been on that cruise and these pictures prove it.

I felt a sudden anger knowing that I had wanted so badly for her to be the woman in those shoes. And felt angrier knowing that she couldn't possibly be.

I headed toward the subway again, feeling more frustrated than any of the nine-to-fivers swirling around me.

Dad interrupted his practice session to come upstairs. I prepared a drink and kicked off my shoes as I explained my latest theory. Perhaps if I verbalized it, talked about it often enough, something—something that had been overlooked—might come to light.

"Chrissie?" Dad looked up from the photos spread like a fan before him. "She was on the ship."

When I didn't answer, he leaned back and scrutinized me with narrowed eyes. "You're not allowing your feelings to get in the way of your judgment, are you?"

"What do you mean?" I asked, knowing very well what he meant, but hoping he'd say something different.

"I'm saying the saleswoman is probably lying."

"About what?"

"I mean, how do we really know that there's only one pair of shoes like this? Salespeople are interested in sales, not in telling the truth. And shoe salespeople are worse than used-car people. You know that yourself, as many pairs of bad-fitting shoes you got talked into buying."

I didn't appreciate the personal comparison and felt a slight rise in my blood pressure. My size 10s were my business but he wasn't finished with his lesson and I had to listen to the bitter end.

"You gotta be extra careful. Who knows? Maybe a hundred pairs of these shoes walking around as we speak. And a whole lot cheaper than six hundred fifty. I'd check and recheck if I were you before saying anything to Ozzie.

"I mean suppose, by some magical power, it *was* Chrissie at the scene? Suppose she knew Travis was involved with Starr? Where's the hard evidence—the fingerprints, the knife that was used? Proof that she was actually in the apartment?

"From where I sit, sounds like one of Stovall's women. Probably trotted up there in a knockoff of these shoes, knocked Starr off, and cut out."

Knocked her off and cut out...

I gathered the pictures from the table and left Dad sitting there. A hole was shot in my theory and I needed to rethink this whole thing. Why would the salesperson have lied? She risked losing an important sale (if I decided not to return). Something wasn't right. Then again, maybe it was my attitude that wasn't right.

I changed into a pair of jeans, collared Ruffin, and stepped out to take him for his nightly walk following the usual route past St. Mark's church to the perimeter of St. Nicholas Park. Minutes later, however, I detoured to Douglass

Boulevard, where the lights from Bert's shop cast a glow over the crowded avenue.

She was alone when I entered and I felt free to sink into the chair near the window and sink further into a pool of despair. Ruffin lounged on the floor at my feet.

"I need a deep conditioner . . ."

Bert heard something in my voice. "You need more than that but it's good for starters. Had a fight with Tad, I bet."

She assembled the shampoo, the towel, and a large bottle of conditioner. "And I bet you lost."

I did not answer. I was not in the mood.

She waved me over to the basin, and the spray of water on my scalp seemed to open up more than my pores. I wanted to cry. Instead I let out a sigh, a whoosh of air that summed up more than losing a fight. It spoke of Ozzie puzzling over Starr's journal. Of Dad, who seemed to be slipping day by day, a breath at a time, into his own state of despondency.

And my own fear. I never thought of my father as being old. But now it was like watching a movie of him and each frame caught a different image—a deeper line across the forehead, under the eyes, near the mouth.

And somewhere near the center of my feelings was my unacknowledged rush to reconfigure a jigsaw puzzle in order to jam certain pieces in where they couldn't possibly fit. I wanted to arrange stuff that would put Chrissie's hand at Starr's throat.

"It's Tad, ain't it?" Bert's voice filtered through the warm spray and I opened my eyes.

My scalp felt light, as if a tight band had been eased away.

"Tad? I suppose so."

"I know so," she said, turning off the spray. She applied a layer of conditioner to my scalp and I was enveloped in the scent of lilac. She slipped a plastic heating cap on my head, covered my shoulders with a thick towel, then headed to the rear of the shop to the coffeemaker.

"Listen, Mali. You ain't got but so much hair. Don't let it fall out over some B.S. Whatever's buggin' you out, talk it out, straighten it out. That's what Franklin and I had to do.

"That hospital thing had really got to me, you know. I mean, suppose somethin' had happened while he was out in the street? Suppose the nurse had peeped in? Or suppose the doc had been ready to run the tests? And him in the wind? Coulda got hit by a bus or somethin' and the docs and nurses and even me would've been wonderin' to this day how the hell an in-patient coulda got hit by a bus."

She poured two cups of coffee and extended one to me. "It's like the old folks say, 'All shut-eye ain't sleep—' "

"—and all good-bye ain't gone," I said, finishing the adage.

"That's right. I told Franklin that he had played a tight game that night. A real tight game. And scared ten years off my life, not to mention his poor mama. But you know, we talked it out so everything's cool now. Now, I ain't tryin' to get in your business, but I think you oughta talk to your man."

I felt a mix of emotions just then: I was happy for Bert and drowning in my own sorrow. She was lucky. Franklin understood her and loved her.

There was a message from Elizabeth when I returned home.

"Mali, some more receipts just came in. I haven't had a chance to go through them yet but you might want to look at them."

The message clicked off and I sat on the edge of the bed and looked at the phone resting in my lap.

I'll speak to Elizabeth later. Right now, I want to speak to someone else.

When I dialed Tad's number and he came on the line, I held my breath, not sure if I wanted to speak after all. Thanks to that damn caller ID, I didn't have to.

"Hello, Mali."

"Hello, Tad."

There was a silence which threatened to stretch significantly so I said, "I need to talk to you about something."

"Come on over. I'll be here."

I hung up and pushed the notes and pictures into my shoulder bag. Then I changed from my jeans to something more suitable, refreshed my face with his favorite lipstick, and left the house.

He offered me a drink but I was too wound up to take it. Boy, did he look good. He smelled good. I wondered if after I had hung up, he had showered and quickly slipped into the pale yellow cotton shirt and those tan linen slacks he knew I liked so much. His hair was combed and the silver seemed to catch like sparks in the soft light of the living room.

I sat on the edge of the sofa trying not to look too hard at him. But a few minutes later, my bubble evaporated.

"So you're coming to me with this. What else do you have?"

"What else like what?" I asked. I had heard something rising from somewhere in the back of his question and the sound sent up a prickle of anger within me. What on earth was the matter with him?

I began to rethink the wisdom of bringing this information to him. Maybe I should've phoned it in to the TIPS hotline and I'd have been ten damn thousand dollars richer. But the scenario was so bizarre they might've laughed it off and not even bothered to file it.

I knew I was taking a chance, knew he would be angry, and would get angrier because I was still not minding my own business, but hell, two lives were gone, another was disintegrating, and my own dad was not doing well either.

Maybe I should have gone straight to Ozzie. But Ozzie had blood in his eye, and one more body wouldn't have solved anything and Dad would've lost a piano man for good. Better to bring it here. After the anger faded, at least Tad would move on it.

But this attitude was more than I bargained for. What was going on?

I decided to go slow, check myself at every comma, because there was no room for two volcanos to explode in the same space.

But when he opened his mouth, my best intentions evaporated and I forgot about the commas.

"So where'd you get this information? While you were out walking Ruffin at three A.M? Did Travis help you figure this out? Did he help you walk the dog? Or help with anything else?"

"Tad, what?"

"You were out pretty late, or should I say early? It must have been some damn deep conversation to make you stroll right on by your own house. And it was a good twenty minutes before you remembered where you lived."

My mouth fell open.

All good-bye ain't gone and all shut-eye ain't sleep.

I stared, trying to decide if I should laugh, cry, or tell him off for allowing his jealousy (the same thing that was aggravating me) to make a world-class fool of him.

But then he pointed a finger at me, wagged his hand in my face, and seemed to be treating me like a suspect in the precinct interrogation room. I stared at him, at that hand, and all I could think of . . . all I could think of . . .

I don't know what I thought. He was shouting and waving the way my mother used to wave, except this man, whom I loved as much as my mother, was not my mother. His voice climbed the scale until I no longer heard it.

"Listen," I whispered through my teeth, "don't wave anything in front of my face that I can't eat!"

"What?"

"You heard me!" I reached into my bag again and threw the rest of the pictures in his face.

"What the hell is this?"

"Pictures. And they don't lie!"

I read his face as he stared at one photo, then another.

"Fold your fingers in your hand and put them in your pocket if you want to keep them. Wave them in my face again and we got a serious problem. Better yet, wave it at that half-naked, over-the-hill-slut that's so hot for you!"

I turned away and headed for the door, not knowing what to expect. If I didn't hear his voice by the time I opened the door, I knew I would not hear it again. Ever. I'd never see him again. That, more than anything, brought the tears. I bit my lip trying to keep them from spilling over, from acknowledging the sorrow, the loss, the void that I could never fill again, but would remain like something large and unquenchable within me.

Reason could not help me now, neither could Mama's presence, as much as I needed her to steady me. Remorse swept in. Why couldn't I have simply asked him to explain the photos? Why couldn't I control myself? Why did I get so damned emotional, why—?

"Mali?"

His voice was soft but strong enough to turn off the noise in my head. When I turned, I saw that his face had softened also, though I could see he was in pain. Whether it was physical or emotional, I couldn't tell. I watched as he moved toward me. The space grew smaller until we were eye to eye, then nose to cheek. Then I felt his mouth moving against the nape of my neck and his arms were around me squeezing so hard, I lost what little breath I had been holding. I heard his voice and felt his breath against my skin. "Girl. Don't you know me by now?"

It was all he said, or at least all I heard or cared to hear. Then I felt the tremor in his chest, shoulders, arms, until it bubbled up, frightening me as laughter broke through.

"What?" I whispered, stepping back, hoping he wasn't on the edge of a nervous break. "What is it?"

"Nothing. Everything," he said, nodding his head. "One of these days I'm going to see the light before I lose you forever."

"That was just a warm-up," I said, trying to calm down myself. "You should see me when I'm angry."

We did not speak then. Instead, we sat on the sofa and I concentrated on the faint cry of a tugboat horn that floated in from the river, filled the silence, then died. The squawk of a gull followed. I thought of stepping out on the terrace but we remained as we were. I heard his deep breathing, the tick of the clock on the shelf above the rows of books, a car fourteen stories below sliding to a halt on bad brakes. I listened intently to these sounds, heard everything except the voice circling in my own head.

What had happened to this relationship? I was ready to beat down Chrissie and he was ready to beat Travis. If it wasn't so damned sad, it would be truly funny. I made an effort and the voice turned off. Win, lose, or draw, I still had to do the right thing.

"The whole thing is there," I said, breaking the silence and pointing to my envelope on the coffee table. "My notes, conclusions, everything."

Then I remembered what Elizabeth had said about negotiating one's way out of a tight spot without making the other guy look bad. Though I didn't know how much worse the other guy could look, what with his face in a frown so tight, you'd think he'd just had his front teeth extracted.

But under normal circumstances, if you can negotiate, you can walk away with your life, your pride, even your love. So I added: "Perhaps there's something, perhaps there's nothing at all."

"We'll see," he whispered.

In the dim light, I saw that his teeth were intact and perfect. Perfectly suitable to leave any mark he wanted on my neck.

"And how about staying for dinner? You'll have to man the burners. The chef is totally emotionally incapacitated."

I stared out Elizabeth's office window at the crowd below and tried not to focus on the previous night. But I still tasted the wine, saw the candlelight, and heard Sade's soft sound. Above all, I heard Tad's sounds when he found he wasn't as emotionally incapacitated as he thought.

But afterward, as I slept, he had gone over the notes and earlier this morning, before he said good morning, before he framed the question, he had shaken his head and I knew what was coming. By now, it sounded as familiar as saying hello.

"You sure you're not allowing your emotions to . . ."

And I had not answered because the evening (except for the photo incident) had gone so well.

So I had listened, biting my tongue, as he outlined the same arguments Dad had laid out. Chrissie was on the cruise. Another woman had the same or similar shoes, and so on.

I had wanted to ask why and how he had come to have so many pictures of her, but he still seemed disturbed about Travis being with me so I decided to wait until we were back on firmer ground.

I reached for the phone and dialed Ozzie. Elizabeth came in and deposited a half dozen credit slips on the table as Ozzie's voice rumbled in my ear.

"Yeah?"

Well, at least he was answering. A great improvement over a week ago so I tried to sound upbeat as I spoke. "Hi, this is Mali. Just called to say that I'll be passing by Charleston's in a minute and thought I'd bring you something. Is that okay?"

"Yeah. Say, that's fine. Look, Mali, I want to apologize for being so rough on you and your dad all this time. You know what I mean, not calling and stuff. Your dad is the best friend I've got and I know I had him kinda worried about me. I didn't mean—"

"I know, Ozzie. I know. No need to say anything."

I hung up, wondering how I was going to talk him into letting me see Starr's apartment. I needed to know if there was something, some small clue that might have been overlooked. I wondered if Ozzie had gone back since the night he had discovered her.

I sifted through the new receipts: an American Express printout of the purchases made on board included a spa treatment, three sweaters from the Cunard Collection shop, champagne at dinner, several liters of duty-free alcohol delivered to her cabin prior to disembarkation in New York, casino chips, laundry service, and several rolls of film. What I was looking for was not on her American Express but another credit card. I held the copy in my hand and studied it carefully.

I need one more thing and it'll pull everything together. I cleared the table and placed the file in the cabinet.

"Still on Chrissie's trail?" Elizabeth said, glancing up as I passed. Her expression told me that she had swelled the ranks of the unbelievers.

"I'm going to see Ozzie," I said, sidestepping the question.

Outside, to my surprise, I found that the weather had finally given us a break. In a matter of a few hours, the sweltering blanket had rolled away and a brisk, cool breeze wrapped around me as I moved under the Apollo Theatre's marquee. At Malcolm X Boulevard, I turned north and strolled to Charleston's, where a slow-moving line stretched to the curb.

Charleston, a few months after he had opened, had cut a small window in the plate glass and from time to time he angled it open. The aroma now spilled out to drift over the crowd, whetting appetites and reminding the impatient ones that no matter how long the wait, it was worth it.

I had suggested that the vent was probably illegal and a cheap marketing ploy.

"So what," he'd said. "Them burners is hot. I need some air."

"How's my piano man?" he now asked when I finally reached the counter.

"I'll let you know later," I said. "One thing for sure, your meals are just what he needs."

His face was wreathed in smiles as he packed an extra order and then pushed the money back toward me.

"Least I can do," he whispered.

When I turned into the block the music flowed toward me, so haunting I hesitated to ring the bell. It seemed like ages since I'd heard his fingers on the keys and now I was afraid to disturb him. I sat on the steps, listening until the last note faded twenty minutes later. Before I could ring the bell, he opened the door.

"Saw you sittin' out there," he said, walking back to sit at the piano. "It's somethin' I'm workin' on. What do you think?"

"It's beautiful, Ozzie. Really beautiful."

"It's for Starr," he murmured, taking the package I extended. "It came to me last night. The notes, the melody, they just came to me about three A.M. and I got up, got myself together, and started puttin' 'em on paper, just started playin'."

"I didn't want it to end," I whispered, "that's why I waited." And for the first time, I thought I saw a trace of a smile.

Charleston had packed so much food, it was easy enough to share everything. But not so easy to say why I had come to visit. I filled two plates with chicken, ribs, sweet potatoes, collard greens, and red rice. We ate in silence until he said, "You know, I was thinkin', I need to go over there. See what's what. Ain't been back since it happened, you know."

I remained quiet and he looked at me and shrugged. "Now's as good a time as any. Gotta do it while I'm in a frame of mind, you know what I mean?"

"You're right," I said, gathering the paper plates and putting them in the trash. Then I grabbed my bag and was waiting at the door when he came back down the stairs. He had changed into a light cotton sweater and a pair of jeans and sandals. He appeared calm but a second later, he brushed his hand over his eyes and drew in a deep breath, as if venturing out was a critical move. I waited, holding the door open and holding my breath, hoping he would not find an excuse to retreat back upstairs.

We avoided the density of 125th Street and chose instead to walk across 124th Street but even on this relatively quiet block, several people recognized him.

We strolled past Rice High School and in the middle of the block, people left their stoops to offer handshakes and condolences:

"Sorry about Starr, Ozzie."

"Man, I'm sorry about what happened. Hope to see you back on track soon."

"Sorry, brother. I'm real sorry."

He hugged a lot, received several pats on the shoulder, and the short distance turned out to be a very long walk.

A half hour later, we sat down on the bench across the street from her house. It had grown dark and the cast-iron frame of the Mount Morris fire watch tower loomed seventy feet above us in the center of the park.

The streetlights blinked on and lights circling the perimeter of the tower also beamed up. I gazed at the octagonal structure and the spiral staircase leading to the covered observatory where the old fire bell hung.

When Harlem had been largely rural, one hundred fifty years earlier, the bell was used as an alarm but it hadn't been used since 1870, when fire alarm boxes were installed.

"You know," Ozzie said, gazing up at the tower, "in 1973, they renamed this park after Marcus Garvey, the black nationalist leader.

"Sometimes I wonder about all these names and places," he went on. "Look how we just strolled across Lenox Avenue, a street now named for Malcolm X, a man the FBI once called the most dangerous man in America. Now he has a movie that makes me stop what I'm doin' to sit down and press my nose to the screen every time it comes on television.

"He died 'cause he was able to dissect the lies that were put on us from the time we stepped ashore dragging those chains.

"He taught us to reread history, so you know he had to be cut loose. Now he has a postage stamp and the only danger is crossing the avenue named after him.

"Marcus Garvey was just as dangerous, you know," he said, pointing over his shoulder at the park. "With that Universal Negro Improvement Association, he led the largest black mass movement this country had ever seen. Who knows where we could've been today if they hadn't deported him.

"He wanted us to take control of our lives and that made him a double threat.

"Today we got a large park, a little history, and not much else. Things ain't changed."

He continued to stare at the bell tower and murmured, "Sometimes I wonder if it's worth it."

"Worth what?" I asked.

"Worth goin' on. Worth tryin' . . . you know, the drugs are still killin' our kids, wipin' out whole families. We—"

"Ozzie, don't. Please don't. Starr wouldn't want you thinking like this. We've always managed to face the odds and beat them. We take on life day by day, and some days are not as good as others. No one expects you to bounce back overnight. You've got to take it slow."

He looked at me in the shadow of the park lights.

"Jeffrey's a lucky man. He got a wonderful daughter. Thanks

for listenin' to me go on and on. I know you already know all this stuff but I was talkin' to keep from thinkin' about what's waitin' upstairs. Behind her door . . ."

He rose from the bench, holding his back as if pain would not give him a break. Then he looked at the key in his hand.

"Now is not the time, Mali. I just can't do it. Not right now. Not tonight. Maybe if folks hadn't stopped me, called her name. Maybe if—"

"But, Ozzie, there might be something in the apartment that was overlooked, something that—"

"No," he said, glancing around. "But you can step in if you want to. And call me later if you want. Let me know what's what."

With that, he dropped the key in my hand and left me sitting there. I watched him move along the sidewalk, in and out of the small pools of streetlight, until he disappeared.

I remained where I was, staring at the cars racing around the traffic circle. I did not want to enter that apartment alone and I watched for him, listened for his footsteps, hoping he would change his mind.

A few minutes passed and I resigned myself. He wasn't coming back. I felt my own resolve draining away and knew if I waited, I wouldn't be going any place but home.

After the forensic team had finished its work, the apartment had been left unsealed. I turned the key in the lock and stepped into the darkened space. The flick of the light switch bathed the living room in a soft, almost romantic ambience and I wished I were stepping in under different circumstances. The Victorian-style furniture made the room seem smaller than it was but Starr had had good taste and the pieces, though not authentic, were well made.

Her image, larger than life, still smiled from the X-slashed poster leaning against the wall, and two chairs were overturned, their cushions scattered across the floor like plump, oversized Frisbees. I wasn't sure if they had been moved during the attack or during the police investigation so I left them where they were.

The stains on the floor near the door had turned black and although they were dry, I avoided stepping on them as I made my way to the center of the room. The stillness unnerved me and I was glad I had left the door unlocked and partly open. Rap music sounded from the apartment near the end of the hall; I needed a connection to the noise of the living.

I heard no movement beyond the living room and knew I was alone. The windows were closed and stale heat, which hadn't circulated for days, now pressed down, almost suffocating me. But even in this hot place, the narrow trickle of perspiration trailing down the small of my back triggered a chill.

I dismissed the feeling and looked around me. The apartment was laid out in a perfect square, and from where I stood in the living room I could see the large bedroom to my left and the kitchen with replicas of old-fashioned appliances—hooded stove, freestanding sink—straight ahead of me.

From the bedroom, a door led to the bathroom. There was also a door leading from the kitchen to the bathroom.

I decided to look into the bathroom first, the bedroom next, then the kitchen, and finally the living room.

The oval-mirrored medicine cabinet held the usual supply of aspirin, toothpaste, Band-Aids, and mouthwash. The claw-foot bathtub had a faint ring, as if Starr had bathed just before she was attacked. She had been found in her bathrobe so she had probably left the bathroom to answer the doorbell.

Ozzie had said the gown she had planned to wear that night had been draped across the chair in the bedroom. It was not there now and I wondered if she had been cremated in it.

The cosmetics on the dresser reminded me of a still life: brilliant red lipstick spiraling up from an uncapped tube. A small jar of face cream. An eyebrow pencil, and several tissues, some faintly smudged with makeup. A wide-tooth comb lying near a brush and an old, Victorian-style gilt-edged hand mirror completed the tableau but told me nothing except I was glad Ozzie had not come in with me. Maybe later, after Dad and I could return and clear away this painful inventory.

The wastebasket near the dresser had been emptied, as had the basket in the bathroom, probably by the investigation unit. All the drawers were opened and clothing hung over the sides. The closet was crammed, and coat pockets already turned inside out.

I saw that the corners of the rug had also been turned back so I returned to the bathroom and stood in the doorway, my gaze sweeping the area near the commode, the tub, the basin, under the basin. Nothing.

I entered the kitchen and looked around. There on the table wedged between the shaking heads of the small Kewpie-doll salt and pepper shakers was a familiar toothpick, hollow plastic, with a sharp point that opened on one end.

Exactly like the delicate picks nestled near the mound of dessert chocolates on the tables in the Queen's Grille, the cruise ship's dining room.

I slipped a napkin under it and rolled it up, humming along with the rap beat that floated in but adding my own words: "Whatcha gonna say when the DNA . . . gotcha on the run and you can't have fun . . . Whatcha gonna do when they . . ."

If the results matched, then Miss Big Hips would soon be swinging them at the guards, some of whom had no taste anyway when it came to prisoners.

The rap beat disappeared, shut off as if a door had been closed. I stood still, a cascade of deep feeling flowing through me:

not fear but intense bitterness. Hatred. Jealousy. Strange emotions capable of draining the soul and the spirit and emptying the mind of rational thought. And capable of making the hair on one's head stand on end in moments of intuition.

I sensed her presence before I actually saw her. When I turned around she was standing in the living room near one of the chair cushions, hands on hips in that familiar pose.

"You make this mess?" she asked pleasantly.

"I was about to ask you the same thing," I replied, stepping into the room to face her. I looked at the size 10 sweater stretched over the size 14 frame and wondered again how the sister managed to draw breath. More important, I wondered if she had a weapon. None was visible but I knew she wouldn't have stepped into a situation unprepared to go the distance.

"So what did you hope to find out by coming on to my husband the other night? Or should I say the other morning?"

Coming on to her husband? I knew folks had been in the street to beat the heat that night but I didn't realize a whole damn parade was trailing me. First Tad. Now her. Who else was on the scene?

"I was trying to tie up some loose ends," I said, watching her hands to make sure they didn't find their way to her jacket. Her boldness let me know she indeed had a weapon, I was certain of that, but what kind, I didn't yet know.

"Tell me," I asked, "were you shading me or your husband?"

"I'll let you figure that out," she said. "And by the way, the saleswoman, Miss Dori? She called to thank me for referring you to the shop. She didn't get your name but she certainly remembered your eyes. Wasn't she thoughtful?"

"Well, what are friends for?" I said, still watching the hands.

She eased closer, maneuvering like a snake intent on finding just the right rock. Her face was like a clown's mask: too much lipstick on too much mouth and enough silver eyeliner to outshine a traffic light. I wondered if she used a mirror when she applied her makeup. With a face like hers, it was no wonder she had been jealous of Starr.

"So how'd you like the black museum?" I asked.

She stopped moving and stared at me. "The what?"

"You know, the black museum. When the ship docked, we all went to visit it. Tad spotted you in the crowd."

His name caught her off guard, seeped through her defenses, and allowed a small smile to break through. "Oh, uh, yes. It was nice."

"Too bad we couldn't catch up with you," I continued.

"I left early," she said, probably holding tightly to the picture of Tad.

"So I gather," I said. "You left Newport early enough on Friday to rent a car, drive back to Harlem, and take care of Starr on Saturday night, then beat tracks back to Newport in time to make the last jazz set on deck. Receipts and signatures don't lie."

Her deep intake of breath threatened to put a serious strain on the sweater but a second later she exhaled. I expected an explosion of denial, a plethora of profanity, outright evasion. Accusations that I had been fooling with her husband. Or that Starr had gotten what she deserved for fooling with the wrong man.

But for a moment, there was only that hush, that tight silence that surrounds a snake before it strikes. Then she whispered, "I knew you were on to something, stepping too close the day you stepped into Travis's store. I knew it. That thing about your man was just a cover. I should've taken care of you myself."

"So you sent somebody?"

"I sent a fool, a fool, and he messed up. But not again!"

The light in the room may have been dim but the flash of that Harlem Equalizer was unmistakable. The blade flicked open at the press of her thumb as she lunged.

This was the moment I had been waiting for. All the energy surged forward when I saw the knife. I didn't wait. I grabbed the knife hand, pulled her forward, and slammed my knee into her midsection.

She blew out a hard breath and crumpled but did not fall. Instead, she staggered backward, swiping the blade in a wide arc, and got me near my shoulder, just missing my neck.

I was still holding on and we grappled like two dancers unsure of our steps, stumbling over the cushions and against the overturned chairs. She outweighed me by at least thirty pounds and her hands were like steel. We fell to the floor, and she rolled over before I did, put a knee in my stomach, and had the blade near my ear.

My hands were at her throat and my thumb was pressed against her windpipe but I couldn't shake the knife loose. She was choking but determined to see my throat cut. Her one knee must have weighed more than I did and I felt my breath leaving me, but I had no intention of dying from anyone's excess weight. Or anyone's knife either.

I grabbed the cushion and pulled it to me as she swung again and the space between us filled suddenly with a cloud of down.

Then I grabbed her hand and bent her wrist back until the knife clattered to the floor. We fought through the feathers. I snatched out clumps of her weave. We slugged it out like two street women brawling over a man. And in a way, I was. How dare she look at Tad the way she did?

With that, I wound up and landed a blow between her eyes that sent her reeling. She hit the floor and, just as quickly, came up again with the knife. But I had the small canister out of my pocket and in my hand. When she came at me, I pressed the button and she dropped the knife, disoriented. This time, when my fist connected, she fell backward over a table and hit the wall. When she went down, she stayed down.

I sank to the floor myself, breathless, but only for a second. I staggered to the bedroom, grabbed several of Starr's belts from the drawer, and by the time Chrissie came to, she wasn't able to move.

31

I've got to break down and get a cell phone. By the time I ran down the hall and persuaded Mr. D.J. to dial 911, Chrissie was screaming loud enough to bring out everyone in the house and some parts of the neighborhood. People stared at me in the hallway as if I had kidnapped her.

Meanwhile, Mr. D.J. was pressing his card in my hand and asking my phone number. "You pretty when you mad," he said, flashing large gold teeth. "And I love mad, pretty women."

I ignored him and called Tad, Ozzie, and my dad. They must have hopped in the same car because they all came through the door at the same time, but everything was under control.

I learned later that Chrissie knew that Travis wanted to leave her for Starr, so she planned the cruise in an effort to reconcile. When he refused, she decided to get Starr out of the way.

The night of the murder, not only had Sno seen her but Short Change had been sitting in his car shadowing Starr and also saw Chrissie leave the house. Short Change approached her a few days later, figuring he had a whore for life as a trade-off for his silence. Instead, she met him near the park and put a bullet in him with her husband's .38. Since Travis was going to leave her anyway, she would blame the murder on him and let him spend the time away from her in jail.

"That's why she wanted so many pictures taken. With my camera," Tad said, trying to mollify me a few nights later.

We were sitting on the terrace, watching the sun spread its last, faint glow over the Harlem River before moving westward.

"That's why she came on the way she did," he said. "She needed a witness to swear that she was on that ship at the time of the crime."

"She nearly got away with it," I said.

"Speaking of shoes," he murmured, looking at my legs. "How much did a pair like that cost?"

I gazed at him in the dying light and saw the rare smile. I smiled back and nodded. "Don't bother. Knowing you, I probably wouldn't have them on that long."